The Dry Well

The Dry Well

Stories

by

Marlin Barton

FREDERIC C. BEIL
SAVANNAH

Copyright © 2001 by Marlin Barton

Published by
Frederic C. Beil, Publisher, Inc.
609 Whitaker Street
Savannah, Ga. 31401

LIBRARY OF CONGRESS CATALOGING-IN-PUBLICATION DATA

Barton, Marlin, 1961–
The dry well : stories / by Marlin Barton
        p.   cm.
Contents: Jeremiah's road–The dry well–A shooting–Conjure woman–
A visitor home–The minister–A father and son–An afternoon at Carter's–
Accusations–Longer than summer–Fires–The cemetery.
ISBN: 1-929490-07-0 (alk. paper)
1. Alabama–Social life and customs–Fiction. I. Title.
PS3552.A7727 D79 2001
813'.6–dc21   00-042925

First edition

This book was typeset by SkidType, Savannah, Georgia;
printed on acid-free paper; and sewn in signatures.

These stories, some in slightly different form, were first published
in the following journals: "Jeremiah's Road," "Conjure Woman," and
"The Minister" in *Shenandoah*; "The Dry Well" in *The Sewanee Review*;
"A Shooting" in *The Virginia Quarterly Review*; "A Visitor Home"
in *Amaryllis*; "A Father and Son" and "An Afternoon at Carter's"
in *The South Carolina Review*; "Longer Than Summer"
in *American Literary Review*; "Fires" in *The Crescent Review*;
and "The Cemetery" in *The Southern Review*.
"Jeremiah's Road" was also published in
Prize Stories 1994: The O. Henry Awards.

For my mother,
Jeannine L. Beinert,
help beyond measure,

and to the memory of
my maternal grandmother,
Jeanne Hazen Beinert

Contents

Acknowledgments

For their help and encouragement, I would like to
thank my teachers James Lee Burke,
Stephen Hathaway, and Philip H. Schneider.
I would also like to thank Rhonda Goff,
Wayne Greenhaw, Janet Peery, Dale Ray Phillips,
Ron Rash, George Singleton, and Susan Tekulve
for their much-needed support and advice.
Further thanks go to Kim Gibby, Eleanor Lucas, and
Capitol Book & News in Montgomery, Alabama.
A final thank-you to the Alabama State
Council on the Arts.

The Dry Well

Jeremiah's Road

HE IS AT IT AGAIN. Jeremiah can't see him, but he hears him and knows that across the old roadbed that is nothing now but a ditch full of trees and brush—but used to carry people on mules and in wagons back in the long ago, carry them all the way over into Mississippi if they wanted to go that far—is that crazy boy walking around the trunk of a great dead white oak, first one direction and then the other, endless circle after endless circle in the dust of that sunbaked dirt yard. And he hollers all the while. Lord, how he hollers.

"Gon' have to kill Luther! This nigger ain't talking! Ain't saying shit! Haa! Beat this nigger!" The sound of the voice is violent. It is a rasp that breaks the quiet into pieces.

Jeremiah is sitting on his porch. He takes a long breath, shakes his head. As often as he has heard Luther, he is still not used to the sound. The hollering makes him nervous, unsettled,

13

as if he is waiting on the bad news that must follow such a commotion. He wonders if maybe Marvin is out there by the tree, too, picking at Luther again. It is always worse when Marvin taunts Luther.

Jeremiah wishes the hollering would stop, and for a moment it does. There is a peaceful silence. He takes another deep breath, feels his stomach settle. He clasps his black hands together, stretches his arms, and rubs his palms. The skin is rough there, dry. Age and work, he thinks. Too many years on God's earth and too many years of ploughing for Conrad Anderson. And not ploughing with no tractor neither. He stops rubbing his hands, holds them out, fingers spread, and looks at them, remembers how they felt on the worn plough handles, how thick the calluses were.

"Hit me again! Haa! Come on!"

In the winter he can see Luther. All the trees are bare and the bushes dead. Now all he can do is hear, but that is more than enough.

He used to go over across the old road and visit about every day, mostly with Verdel, but with the children, too, and then grandchildren. So many of them living there together. But Verdel has been dead for four years, and there are great-grandchildren now. And sometimes strangers. Faces he doesn't know and doesn't want to know. Mean faces from far away.

Luther is the youngest of Verdel's children. He has, besides Marvin, ten brothers and sisters and half-brothers and half-sisters, some still at home, some that Jeremiah hasn't seen in a long, long time. They are scattered. Up North. The same place where those strangers come from, where Marvin, and then Luther, came back from.

Jeremiah remembers when Luther was a wide-eyed little boy who could barely walk. And he remembers how Luther grew so fast and how he gave him pieces of penny candy, peppermint and gum, and little hard cookies until Luther got too old for that. "Tell Jeremiah 'Thank you,' Luther," Verdel would say. The little boy would grin and, like so many children, hide his face in his mama's skirt. Then, as Jeremiah would get up and start out across the old road, Luther would come up suddenly, grab his leg, and say, "Thank you."

"Vietcong gon' have to kill Luther! Luther ain't talking. Haa!"

Vietcong, nothing, Jeremiah thinks. Detroit. Nothing but Detroit and that dope. Ain't been nowhere but Detroit. Jeremiah has never been there, never been more than thirty miles from the house where he was born, but he knows about that place. Making cars and taking dope. Drive down here with that stuff, get a poor country nigger on it. Shuck! Didn't used to be.

He remembers when things started to change. Verdel was still alive, but sick so much she couldn't rule the roost like she once had. And Marvin, after so many years, had come back down from Detroit, away from his father. He was no longer that little boy who used to play down by the creek and show Jeremiah the mussels he dug up out of the sand. Marvin had a surly look about him. He was quiet, carried himself in a kind of slouch, and barely moved, except when he was beating on Luther or one of the grandchildren. It wasn't playful fighting, like brothers do; it was mean. His sleepy eyes would open wide, and his arms would swing wild as he hit and slapped.

It is beginning to get dark now. The shadows are gone, melted into each other with the last of the sun's heat. The smell of evening comes. It is clean and a little cool, a trace of moisture in it, but not sticky as in the day. This is Jeremiah's favorite time. He lets the coolness settle on him like dew and thinks of the old days, remembers coming in from work about this time. He would have been chopping cotton, or if it was after Mr. Conrad quit planting he might have been getting a cow up or checking on a newborn calf. Even now, when he walks through the pasture to pay Mr. Conrad his rent, he likes to look over the young calves. They are so wide-eyed and spirited.

"Luther ain't talking! Kill this nigger. Put me in the ground!"

"Lord," Jeremiah whispers.

He looks up and sees Mary and Rosa coming home. They are young with pretty brown skin and tight shapes. They live in the other side of his house. Sometimes one or the other will sit out and talk with him, most times not. Mary has an older brother who comes and takes Jeremiah to Demarville to cash his check the third of every month. It is almost time again. Verdel used to make Marvin take him, but it wasn't long before she couldn't get him to do it anymore. He just got too sullen. Marvin used to tell him that he ought to put his money in the bank. "It my business what I do," he would tell Marvin.

The girls stop at the edge of the porch. Mary says that they have been up to the store and that it is a right nice evening, not too hot. They going to fix them some supper now she says. They climb the steps and go inside. He watches them.

He sits awhile longer. He doesn't hear Luther anymore. The spell has maybe worn off him for now, let him alone. He has probably gone inside, had enough of walking in circles for this day. Jeremiah sees again Luther's little-boy face, the wide eyes like a calf's, the shy smile. And he thinks about all the trips Luther has made up North the last several years. Gone for six months at a time. "Lord," he calls out. He hopes that maybe Luther will soon be asleep. He figures that it is only when Luther sleeps that his mind quits talking to him, at least where he can hear.

It is dark now. He sees the electric light shining out of Rosa and Mary's windows. It breaks through the rusted screens and strikes the gray, worn boards of the porch. When Mr. Conrad finally put electricity in the house, Jeremiah told him that he didn't want it. "No, sir! A coal-oil lamp all I need." He even had to argue, and was afraid Mr. Conrad would put electricity in anyway. But he didn't. Jeremiah likes the soft light that the flame from the wick puts out, the way the light is gently absorbed by the dark wood walls. There is a kind of glow, a luster, that is a constant in his mind. He can look at the lamp at night and remember the same light from his earliest memories. The light even has a smell to it that is gentle and so familiar. It eases him, and so often now he does not feel easy. He isn't sure why. He sometimes in the night feels as if he is lost out in deep woods, and the thing that bothers him most is that he knows they are the woods that he used to hunt in and know so well. He killed deer there, and squirrels, and hunted coons.

He gets up, walks inside, and pulls the screen door to, latching it. His room is hot, and he leaves the heavy door open. There isn't much breeze, but he wants to catch what little might come along. He has his windows open.

He undresses in the dark, washes his face over a wash-pan, and lies down on the bed. From there he can see the small fireplace and his chifforobe and a cane-bottom chair. The room has a dank smell to it that is also familiar. It pushes down on his senses. He can taste it, feel it on his skin.

After he has rested a minute he slides himself to the bed's edge, reaches underneath, feels for cool metal, and pulls the .32 out to where it is right on the floor beside him. This has become one of his two nighttime rituals, the rituals he started when that low, uneasy feeling first began to come down on him. He doesn't know now when that was exactly. Four years ago? When Verdel died? Before that? He isn't sure. But something has come on him, a kind of uneasiness, fear even. A kind of night fear, like a child might have. Not a fear of any man or woman, something more than that, larger. But not death. Just something. As if he is lost out in those woods. Or as if maybe that old road has grown up so thick with trees and brush that he can't tell anymore where he lives. The old marks all gone. And he is just trying to get back to—somewhere.

He moves back onto the middle of his bed and begins his other ritual. He lets himself go limp, stares up at the ceiling, lets the darkness clear his mind, and waits for the old voices and the memories that go so far back. His father's voice is first tonight. And, for the first time in a long while, he hears it clearly. It sounds like it is supposed to, deep and full. "Don't you be going down there to Dawes Quarter. You stay away from them Dawes niggers. They sorry! I catch you down there, boy, I beat you. Better hear me good!"

And now his mother's voice, so gentle. "You leave him alone. He a good boy. He ain't going to get in no trouble. Now is you, Jeremiah?"

He remembers how dark his father's skin was, darker than his, dark as the blackened fireplace bricks. And he remembers the scars on his father's hands where the skin seemed to have boiled up and hardened. He remembers his mother's hands, too, such long brown fingers, the skin so much softer than it should have been for the work she did out in the fields. "How come your skin so soft, Mama?" he'd ask. "It my secret," she would say, and laugh.

He stretches. He is tired and can feel sleep coming on.

The only sounds are those of crickets and sometimes a night bird calling from a long way off.

"Jeremiah! Jeremiah!" His brother's voice now. He sees the little boy sitting on the floor. What does he want? To be carried? He picks him up, takes him outside under the long shade of the sycamore, and lets him play there with a stick. They take turns scratching with it in the dirt. Jeremiah draws shapes, circles and squares, and his brother scratches through them.

How long has that been now? And when exactly was it that his brother died? Had the little boy gotten big enough where he could run, or was it before that? He used to know, but he disremembers now. And when was it that the first house burned? He can see the flames, hear the house falling in on itself. He can hear his mother's cries, her calling out to the Lord, like she did in church, like he does now sometimes. Was the fire before his father fell and missed work? Sometimes he disremembers when things happened back in that long ago, and when he can't make the memories come back right, he feels sick inside, dizzy in his mind.

All dead, he thinks. And Pauline, his wife, took so long ago now. It is her voice that he always waits to hear. Some nights it comes, some nights it is too late in the coming.

He listens, lets his mind go back. He thinks that maybe there is still time tonight. And then: "We have more," he hears. "The Lord took this one, Jeremiah, but there be more. I promise you. Look at all the ones my mama done had. I her daughter ain't I? I tell . . ."

Now that *other* sound. He has waited for it. It pounds through the wall; it wails; its voices shout. Rosa and Mary sing with it, and it takes his mind over and steals the people and places he has known. "Shuck!" he says. There is nothing now but the room's darkness and that awful sound filling up his mind.

He starts to get up, but lies still. He thinks of the old road. He wishes sometimes that he could leave his house and his few things behind and walk down it, pick his way through the trees and brush until he can go no farther.

"Kill this nigger! Put him in the ground," he hears, or thinks he hears, but how can he above the music?

"Open up this door again, bitch! Don't slam no door in my face."

In the first moment that Jeremiah is awake he thinks he hears his father. But the words aren't his father's, and he soon recognizes the voice. Marvin's. There is no music now, just shouting.

"Go on now! We ain't letting you back in. You didn't act right last time."

"Damn you! You know you owe Marvin. Brung you that stuff other night. I seen how it done you. Done you right. Now you can do me right!"

"You acting crazy. Leave us alone! We don't want you around tonight. You wild. Messed up."

Jeremiah has risen from the bed and is standing now behind the screen. Marvin can't see him and Jeremiah waits. He is ready. The room is dark, but at this moment he is sure of everything around him, as sure as the feel of the weight in his right closed hand.

"Fuck you, then! I don't need none of you." Marvin steps back from the door and leans against a post. He stands quiet, waiting, Jeremiah knows, to see if the door will open. Jeremiah waits too. There is no sound. He remembers how Marvin used to beat Luther, how he moved when he hit, how his face narrowed in mean concentration. He knows that Marvin is concentrated on the door now in the same way.

In a few minutes Marvin turns quietly and slips off the porch and through the brush. Jeremiah is surprised; he thinks Marvin would have had more patience. Jeremiah was ready to wait all night.

Morning. He awakens and his first thought is of cotton, long rows of it stretching not-yet-white around the side of a gentle sloping, but terraced, hill. And then he thinks of Marvin and last night and feels a tenseness in himself like he usually feels only when Luther has been hollering half the day. He wonders for a moment how his own child might have turned out. Better than Marvin he likes to think. Pauline said there would be more, but there weren't.

He hears morning sounds: birds and a cow lowing, then the tractor and bushhog out in the pasture. That new boy, he thinks. Mr. Conrad done hired him another one. Reckon how long he last? Didn't even show up Monday.

The tractor sputters, rattles. He looks out his window and sees gray smoke shoot up every now and then above the machine. Mr. Conrad tried to get him on that thing so many times after he bought it. Had even cussed him once. The same thing happened when Mr. Conrad bought a lawn mower with an engine. Jeremiah just sharpened the blades on the old one and went to work.

He dresses, puts on his hat, and picks up his walking stick. The wood is worn smooth with handling. He walks to the county road and turns toward Riverfield. As usual, he doesn't use his stick to help him walk. He holds it crossways behind his back and catches the ends of it in the crook of each arm. It braces him, holds him. The young ones ride by sometimes, say, "Look at Jesus on his cross."

It is a long walk, but he finally gets to the little gathering of buildings. He stops at the post office first, picks up his check, puts it in his pocket, then walks on over to Mr. Conrad's store.

He walks inside and sits in a chair by the window. Miss May, Mr. Conrad's wife, is working today. She is sitting, resting for the moment. She runs a file across her nails. The store is quiet now, but a crowd will soon gather, the way it always does on check day. Mr. Conrad brings him a Coke. "How you feeling this morning, Jeremiah?"

"Fine," he says.

Mr. Conrad gets the things Jeremiah calls out: cheese, rag bologna, a can of peas. He charges these things. Tomorrow, after Jeremiah has cashed his check, he will come and pay his bill. He doesn't let Mr. Conrad cash his check. Mr. Conrad don't need to know everything. A man has a right to keep some things private.

"Have your bill ready for you in the morning, Jeremiah."

"Yes, sir," he says.

He picks up his bag, walks out of the store, and hears the screen slam shut behind him. Several cars pull up to the store the moment he steps out. A crowd stands now in front of the post office. Check Day in Riverfield is beginning. He walks in front of the post office, headed in the direction of home. Sud-

denly Marvin steps out of the crowd and in front of him, looking at him with cat's eyes that seem as if they have just opened
from sleep. Marvin runs his hands down into his pockets,
throws his head back, and rolls a toothpick from one corner of
his mouth to the other. Part of Jeremiah wants to laugh at Marvin's strutting.

"You need to go to town today, don't you, old man? Yeah, I
remember how Mama used to make me take you. 'Be nice,' she
said. Shit."

Jeremiah doesn't speak. He stares past Marvin on down the
road. He tightens his grip on the cane that he has shifted to his
right hand. He waits.

"Tell you what Marvin gon' do for you. I gon' open my taxi
service. That's right. You be my first customer today. For ten
dollars and gas, I take you to Demarville. Let you cash your
puny check. I know you don't be cashing it in there," he says,
pointing to the store.

"Don't want nothing from you," Jeremiah says. He stands
firm, feet planted solid. He waits.

Marvin laughs, then walks away, still laughing.

He is halfway home now. Two cars pass. He steps out of the
way and into the tall weeds beside the road. Both cars blow by
him in a fury of noise and hot wind. Later, another comes
down the road, slower this time, and he hears the steady
thump, thump, thump of loud music, and when it's close, the
shouting voices and all that racket. Nate Johnson's boy, he
thinks. Shuck!

He remembers other music, when he was a boy. A man
sitting out on some porch with a guitar. Whose porch, though?

he wonders. His own? The man makes the sound come out of that wooden box with the blade of a pocketknife. The music is painful-like, as if he uses that knife to cut the sound loose from those shining metal strings. The man plays so slow it seems as if the whole world is still. The wind doesn't even blow. When he puts his guitar down Jeremiah begs for more until his father tells him to *hush*.

Home isn't far now. He turns down the dirt road, sees a car parked beside his house. The old road used to run somewhere right along here, but he can't tell exactly where now. The trees are so thick. He can see it in his mind though. Black folks walking to and from town, someone riding a mule. A white lady in a buggy.

He gets home. Mary's brother, Henry, says, "Was wondering where you was."

"You a little early."

"I reckon so."

Jeremiah goes inside, puts his things away. Henry will take him to Demarville. Jeremiah wants to get his business taken care of.

He sleeps; it's late afternoon. He has been to town, come home, and eaten his lunch of cheese and bologna and black-eyed peas. He usually sleeps about this time. The afternoons are quiet, sometimes quieter than the nights. But today he is awakened suddenly, startled from sleep by a machine-gun sound. And then that violent pouring of words:

"Shoot me! Haa! I ain't talking. Kill this nigger. Kill Luther!"

The Fourth Day, he thinks. They done started already. It ain't even until tomorrow.

He gets up, walks out onto the porch. He hears laughing, boyish squeals from over across the way. More firecrackers explode. He walks down into the old road, slips up to the fence that runs along the other side of it, and watches. He sees Luther, walking silent now around that oak, and the grandchildren and great-grandchildren. Marvin is among them, lighting the fuse and then running back with the rest of them, playing like a kid, as if maybe he never went off up North and came back all mean, messed up. Jeremiah remembers for a moment how he came on Marvin once down by the creek. He saw him all of a sudden, as he did this morning. Only Marvin was just sitting there, peaceful-like, on a sandbar, his legs folded, looking at the water. "What you doing, Marvin?" he said. "Just thinking," Marvin answered. That was all, "Just thinking." He said it so peaceful-like. His eyes were closed. Jeremiah watched him a moment, then walked on off. Let him be. Maybe Marvin got troubles, he thought.

Now, across the fence, he sees those strange faces. Detroit faces. There are usually a few of them around, come to stay with Marvin and Luther. They worse than any Dawes Quarter nigger ever thought about being, he thinks. And Marvin right in there with them.

There are more strange faces than usual. It will be that way all over Riverfield, Jeremiah knows. All the ones that went off to Akron and Cleveland and Chicago come home for the Fourth Day with strange wives and husbands and children. And the ones that left act so different now. Ain't never should have left.

The door to Verdel's old house opens, and Jeremiah stares in amazement at what he sees. It is as if he is looking at someone who has just left the ground of his own accord. A white boy steps from out of the house. He has long blond hair and wears a white shirt and white pants. A regular vision of white in the afternoon sun. What he is doing there Jeremiah can only wonder. Can't be good, he thinks.

All the rest of the afternoon he hears them. Fireworks keep going off; sometimes there is only a single explosion and then quiet, sometimes twenty or thirty go off in rapid bursts and drive Luther into fits. *"Kill me,"* he hollers. *"Luther don't tell nothing!"*

Later Jeremiah hears the racing of a car engine. The sound starts off low and full; then when the engine is gunned it builds in fat spurts until there is nothing but the continual explosion that whines higher and higher, unbearably, through the trees and rises above the old road.

Jeremiah rubs his hands together, rocks his body quickly back and forth in his chair out on the porch. That uneasiness has crept into him and rises through his body. The night fear. He walks inside, even closing the heavy door, but he can still hear the sound and it is too hot to close the windows. He splashes water on his face, but the water is hot against his skin. It runs down his neck and makes his shirt stick.

He walks back outside, down the steps, and over into the road. He peers through the brush and sees a car with its hood up. It's blue, an older make. The white boy and someone black with a fat stomach and no shirt on lean over the engine while Marvin sits behind the wheel and revs the motor, cussing when it idles low. Marvin stomps the gas pedal and turns and looks straight at Jeremiah. For a moment Jeremiah is afraid he's been seen. He waits, but Marvin's face shows no recognition.

Luther walks silent for now. It is Jeremiah who feels like yelling above the sound of the engine.

No music tonight. Mary and Rosa have gone out. The fireworks continually break the quiet, and Jeremiah can't sleep. He feels somehow as if he is waiting on something. Worst of all tonight, the old voices don't speak. Jeremiah strains, listens, sends his mind back, but hears nothing. Seems as if there is nothing there inside him.

The fireworks stop for a moment, and without the voices there is only silence. He doesn't listen for them any longer. He feels the night fear in himself, and he waits for something else now as he lies on top of his quilt, something silent, something that he can't even imagine. He feels heavy, as if something's pushing down on top of him.

He awakens from a dream. Pauline was sitting before him, right there in the cane-bottom chair, pulling apart the seam of an old cloth sack that she wants to use. He hears the tearing sound again. Only it's rougher this time. A creaking now, like the branches of pines in a strong wind. A shadow moves past. And another. Then not a shadow at all but a flash of white, and he raises up, knowing and gasping suddenly for the breath that is like a thick fluid now. This is no dream. A hard weight lands against him. He chokes and then feels a blow against his face, feels his cheek become hot, and tastes the blood as it flows into his mouth in rivlets. "Don't kill him, don't kill the bastard!" he hears. Not a voice he knows. The hot dark body is on top of him, holding him. He remembers his pistol. It's lying there in the dark on the floor—loaded, ready, and so useless now. "Look in the chifforobe," another voice shouts. He doesn't know this one either. The white boy moves quick at the command. He is opening the chifforobe, rifling through it. He looks underneath, finds the metal box. Jeremiah knows how much he's about to lose. He tries to raise up again. Something metal strikes the back of his head. A hand grabs his face, palm in his mouth, and it pushes his head into the pillow. He can't breathe. He tastes the skin, it's full of grease, and bites into the slick flesh like an animal tearing meat. A scream. Two more blows against his head. "You old son of a bitch!" "Don't kill him! Come on," he hears, and the hulking weight is off him. The torn screen door slams and footsteps strike the porch; then he hears a slapping sound, nervous laughter, and then nothing. He shakes, his head is filled with dizziness. He feels lost for a moment, as if he is gone too far out into those woods again and can find his way only if he stumbles onto a familiar landmark, an old dead tree, a creek maybe, or an old road. He takes hard breaths. His lungs are still filled with liquid. The whole thing seems as if it lasted no longer than his dream. He looks to the cane-bottom chair, as if he will find Pauline there. He sees it lying overturned.

He opens the gate, almost stumbles, then walks on through. Mr. Conrad's lights aren't on. He chains the gate back and walks to the house, makes his way up onto the neatly kept porch. Two chairs and a bench sit among potted plants. He knocks several times, then leans against the door frame. He has made up his mind about what he will say. Sometimes you got to lie to tell the truth, he thinks.

He thought about going after them, following them through the trees and bushes in the old road. But he felt too dizzy and weak, felt as if he never would have made it up out of the old road without falling. So he rested, waited until his head cleared. But now, knocking on Mr. Conrad's door, he feels as if he should have stumbled after them. And if he couldn't make it, then so be it. He could die in that road. Ain't got long to live, anyway.

A light comes on and a door opens. Miss May is standing there in a robe; one hand holds it closed. A black hairnet covers her gray hair.

"What's happened, Jeremiah?"

From her expression he knows how bad he must look. He can still taste blood on his lip, and he catches the bitter taste of grease on his tongue every now and then.

"I been robbed, Miss May."

Her sleepy eyes seem to focus, and she looks frightened for a moment.

"Come inside," she says. "I'll get Mr. Conrad."

"No, ma'am. I stay out here on the porch," he says. He feels suddenly dizzy.

She looks at him for an instant, as if to say, "You ought to come on in," then turns and walks back into the house. "It's Jeremiah," he hears her say.

In a moment Mr. Conrad is there, standing in a blue robe. He opens the screen door. "Come in the house, Jeremiah. You been hurt."

"No, sir. I just set right here," he says. But Mr. Conrad holds the screen open still, and he can see Mr. Conrad begin to get aggravated the way he did when he found out that Jeremiah wouldn't drive the tractor. He cuts his eyes, frowns. "Come in where it's cool," he says. Jeremiah steps inside. "We'll get you a chair in the kitchen."

"No, sir," Jeremiah says. He could make it into the kitchen, but he sits down on the floor beside the door.

"All right, then," Mr. Conrad says. "Whatever you want."

Miss May comes back, followed by their son and grandson. The son, who is also named Conrad, is already dressed, and the grandboy, Seth, looks as if he's walking in his sleep. The four of them stand over Jeremiah, peer down at him. He hadn't wanted all this.

"How bad does your head hurt you, Jeremiah?" Miss May asks.

"It be all right."

"We'll call the doctor."

"I just want me some water."

"Don't you want the doctor to look at you?" she says.

"No'm," he says, and turns away.

"I'll get you some water, then." She walks into the kitchen.

Mr. Conrad and his son, who Jeremiah remembers as a little boy, ask at the same moment: "Who did this to you?" Their looks are grave, as if to say, "We will take care of this. Tell us who. Give us a name."

Jeremiah shuts his eyes. He thinks about what he has decided to say, remembers the blows against his head. He opens his eyes, looks at Mr. Conrad and then at his son. They are waiting. The grandboy stands behind them, waiting also, waiting to see what his father and grandfather will do about this. Jeremiah draws a breath slowly until it fills him.

"Marvin, Verdel's boy," he says, then looks blankly at his old, dry hands that hang limp between his knees.

The sheriff comes in a little while. Jeremiah hears the car pull up, and Mr. Conrad and his son tell him they will be right back, then walk outside. They leave the door open. He hears another car; a door slams. He listens for voices, but can't make them out. Finally there are footsteps on the porch, and he hears the words "old man." He closes his hands, tightens them into fists, and remembers how they held the plough.

Mr. Conrad leads the sheriff inside. The sheriff is black. A white state trooper is with him.

"Tell the men what happened, Jeremiah," Mr. Conrad says.

He tells them how he woke up, how one of them held him down while the white boy got his money. Then tells them that he saw Marvin, heard his voice clearly.

"One of them was white?" the sheriff asks.

"Yes, sir. They was all over at Verdel's old house today. I seen them. Some strange black boys and that white boy. They was working on a car."

"What kind?" the trooper asks.

"Blue. Looked like one Miss May used to have awhile back. A Chevrolet, I believe. If I saw it again, I'd know it."

They go first to Verdel's old house. Jeremiah rides with the sheriff; the trooper is behind them, then Mr. Conrad and his son in a pickup. They pull up along side each other in the dirt yard. Jeremiah is sure that the ones who robbed him are long gone. The house is dark, but a dusk-to-dawn lamp shines from a pole.

"Any of these cars the one you saw them working on?"

"No, sir."

The sheriff gets out of the car, tells Jeremiah to stay put. The trooper and Mr. Conrad and his son follow the sheriff to the door. Jeremiah watches the four men. Suddenly he feels a tiredness come on him that is so complete he has to work to catch his breath. He feels as if he has been ploughing all day in the hot sun without a break, or as if he has been walking lost in the woods, walking one circle after another, trying to draw breath from the hot still air.

"Come on out here," he hears the sheriff say. One of Verdel's grandchildren steps out of the door, a girl of about fifteen. Jeremiah can't recall her name. She holds her arms wrapped around her middle, looks at her feet. She doesn't look once at Jeremiah sitting in the lighted car.

"Where's Marvin?" the sheriff says.

A window at the end of the house is opened a little wider. Jeremiah hears it being raised. A hand reaches out, hangs off the sill.

"Tell us where your brother is," the trooper says. "We need to talk with him."

"He my uncle, and I don't know where he at. I ain't see'd him."

"Jeremiah says he saw him over here today," the sheriff says.

She still does not look toward the car. "I ain't see'd him. He gone."

"He take a white boy with him?" the sheriff says. "A couple of black boys?"

"They was some people visiting, but they gone now. They might done headed back up North."

"With Marvin?" the trooper asks.

"Don't know. Don't think so."

"All right then," the sheriff says.

"*Luther ain't talking! Ain't saying shit!*" The voice comes exploding out of the window. "*Gon' have to kill this nigger! Haa!*"

"Don't mind him," Mr. Conrad says. "He's just crazy."

❧

The sheriff and Mr. Conrad decide they should try the Loop Road. They pass across the highway, follow the rough blacktop as it curves past shotgun houses and houses built out of cement block. They drive down into Jackson Quarter, where small shacks crowd winding dirt roads. Jeremiah doesn't see the car.

Back out on the Loop they pass what Jeremiah knows are soybean fields. He has never worked in a soybean field. People didn't used to plant them, but a family came from way off, bought this piece of land that used to grow cotton, and planted beans. Jeremiah thinks now about how he used to fill his sack out in the cotton field beside his mother and father. That life is so long ago to him at this moment that it feels as if it's out of some old book that no one reads from anymore.

They turn left around the Loop, toward Bethel Hill. At the base of the pine-covered slope they approach a trailer in a small clearing. Another dusk-to-dawn lamp shines in the yard. Places lit that never used to be, Jeremiah thinks. He sees the rusted trailer door standing open, and then sees the car, and just as quickly the uneasiness hits him again, that feeling that has slowly taken him over these last years.

"There it be," he says.

The sheriff stops the car suddenly, pulls off the road and into the yard. The trooper and Mr. Conrad follow. Their headlights strike the aluminum, and then each driver turns parallel to the trailer. Jeremiah watches as the trooper leaves his car, runs quickly along the edge of the woods, and, pistol drawn, disappears behind the trailer. Jeremiah hasn't even had time to open his door.

The sheriff and Mr. Conrad and his son are already out, too, standing behind their car and truck, pistols out. Jeremiah finally gets out of the car, stands and watches these men as they call out to Marvin. His chest aches and his legs are weak.

A light comes on in the trailer, and Marvin steps up to the door. He holds his hands out in front of himself. His face is caught for a moment in the light from the dusk-to-dawn lamp, and Jeremiah can see absolutely no trace of fear in the narrowed, hard-set features.

"What you want?" he says.

"Who else is in there?" the sheriff says.

"Just Robert Jackson."

"Tell him to come on out."

"He asleep."

"He ain't no more! Now come on out of there. Tell the others, too."

"Ain't no others."

"I said tell them!"

"We's the only ones. What I done? I been here all night."

"Jeremiah says different," Mr. Conrad says.

"Who? Jeremiah? What that old man say?"

"Come down the steps, *now*," the sheriff says.

Marvin walks down as easily as if he is headed out for a night in Demarville. He is followed by a small wiry man who steps much more slowly and carefully. In a moment the trooper walks through the door. "They weren't lying. Nobody else here."

"All right," the sheriff says. "Robert, you just stay back where we can see you."

The sheriff walks up to Marvin now, puts Marvin's arms behind his back, and handcuffs him, then tells him his rights. He walks Marvin to the car and pushes him into the back seat. Marvin's head strikes the car's top.

Jeremiah stands behind the car. The sheriff leaves the door open, walks over and talks with the trooper and Mr. Conrad and his son. They have done all this, Jeremiah thinks. They have taken care of it all. He feels tired again. His arms are weak and his legs are simply numb now. Is this all? he wonders. "Hey old man," Marvin says. "What you tell them? That I robbed you? Well, fuck you!"

He doesn't speak. He feels the fear that comes on him at night. The kind of fear a man might have if he was bound and blindfolded and set out on some unfamiliar ground, alone. A car passes and, for a moment, he thinks about the old road, sees it as it used to be, the old wagon ruts, the dried manure, sees himself walking on it, headed home. He knows it will lead him there. He wants to go home. He turns toward Marvin. His hand grips hard the cool metal deep in the pocket of his overalls. He moves toward the opened door, feels the weight of the metal in his now extended right hand. Above the shouts of the other men, above Marvin's curses, he hears only one voice, Luther's. *Gon' have to kill this nigger!*

The Dry Well

HE FOUND THE DARKNESS gathered around him as thick as the pines in which they were camped, but after Rafe Anderson blinked once, then twice, his eyes focused on the movement of the pine tops as they raked against the night sky. He saw beyond them the moon, perfect in its half symmetry. Its edge looked as if it had been cut with a knife honed on a fine-grained whetstone; the few streaks of clouds below it gave almost the suggestion of blood, as if the cut had done the moon injury. Rafe had hoped for a night this clear.

He slipped out from beneath his blanket, stood up, and quietly buckled on his belt. Getting past the sleeping men and the horses wouldn't be a problem. If anyone woke, they'd think he was up only to relieve himself. But their waking was not all that likely. They'd been riding for days, and that afternoon they'd taken two hogs off a farm. When the old farmer came walking up, a starved mongrel dog behind him—the two of them clearly related in their poverty—the captain had tried to pay the man in Confederate money, but the farmer had only laughed at the sight of the bills. "Worthless," he'd said. They took the hogs and had the best meal any of them had eaten for at least a month. And now, with the hard riding in their muscles and the meat in their bellies, they stood little chance of waking—unless they heard firing from one of the pickets.

It was the pickets who gave him his only pause as he walked now past the horses. If they saw anyone slipping out, they would shoot. Those were their orders, and he'd seen them followed. In fact, he had carried out those same orders on one occasion. Three desertions three nights running had been too many. It had to be stopped. He'd seen the man, who looked more like a shadow than anything, creeping out of the brush; and, praying it wasn't someone he called a friend, he made himself squeeze the trigger on his carbine. He could not have said then, or now, if he had meant to hit the man. All he remembered was the tightening in his stomach, the simple squeeze of his finger, and the quiet thud the man's body had made when it hit the ground. At least it hadn't been someone he'd known.

The few pickets here wouldn't pose that much of a problem for him. After they'd ridden east out of Hillsborough, he'd begun to recognize farms and houses. It was as if the old images escaped from his brain and appeared before him, no longer painted on the canvas of his memory, but fully realized. Now they were just outside of Durham. He hadn't seen these farms since years before the war, but he knew them well, just as he knew these woods he had hunted in as a boy.

And now he found the ravine, that old deep scar in the ground, just where he'd remembered it. He breathed heavy with relief, slipped down its side quietly, and walked through the pines and scrub cedars. The sharp smell of resin was strong in the air.

After a few hundred yards, well past the pickets, he crawled up the steep bank, pulled himself over the top, then checked to see that his cap-and-ball revolver and bowie knife, the same knife he'd once pulled on a highwayman years before, were still secured to his belt. He began walking slowly toward the road. The woods were thinner here. Instead of thick pine groves, hardwoods such as white oaks and sweet gums grew tall, and their shade kept scrub from growing up. Squirrel-hunting had always been good here. He remembered how his father would shake a vine and he and his brothers would shoot, each of them wanting to lay claim to the most killed.

Once he made the main road, he would follow it just inside the tree line. There was risk. It was always possible that a Federal patrol was near. He figured he had about a three-mile walk, if he remembered the landmarks right, and he was sure that he did.

He didn't know exactly why he was taking this chance. Perhaps it was simply because he felt the pull of home and blood, felt it stronger now than he had in years. He was so close. Nine years, almost ten, he'd been gone, six of them before the war had begun. All the traveling he'd done since he'd joined had never brought him this close before, and he felt as if he'd been about everywhere there was to go: Virginia, Tennessee, Georgia, Mississippi. And Alabama, of course, where he'd enlisted— over in Demarville.

He'd made the road now and was walking along its shad-owed edge. Every few steps he would stop and listen for riders, ready at any moment to drop quietly to the ground. A thin layer of sweat covered his face, but when the wind blew he felt suddenly cool. Another mile or so and the road would fork; then he'd follow the deep ruts of the left branch and that would take him almost there.

The last time he'd walked this road had also been at night, only then the moon had been full and its light almost enough for coon hunters not to even need a lantern. He'd spent the first part of the night hiding down in the old well; the darkness in that hole had been so thick he felt he could touch it. It seemed strange that a man could carry an image of nothing but blackness in his brain, but he had ever since his stay in that well. After enough hours had passed, certain that everyone, even his father, was asleep, he'd climbed out, crept into the house, gath-ered a few of his things, and left. He'd been fifteen years old then and so full of fear that, despite the moonlight, he could barely see the road he walked on.

He was beginning to cover some ground now, but he moved slowly. He knew there was a creek nearby, and he tried to listen for it as it ran over the small dam he and his brothers had built, but he couldn't make it out. He even stopped for a moment. He remembered how cool and clear the water was and how he and his brothers and sister used to play in it when the weather was hot. But maybe he was wrong. Maybe he wasn't as close to it as he thought. He began walking again, still half listening for its sound.

After that night in the well, he'd traveled a week, stealing food out of gardens, and then in the town of Pittsboro he'd met an uncle who had once been in jail and who was no longer mentioned by anyone in the family. The uncle, without any questions, had given him money and a slave by the name of March Whitney. He traveled south, down into Georgia, working and hiring out March as he went. Twice he had to fight grown men who tried to rob him and take March. He'd pulled his knife on one of the men and cut him deep across his shoulder. Each time he'd kept his money, and March. By the time he reached West Alabama, after a year and a half of traveling, he decided he'd come far enough. The Alabama Black Belt was rich, both the soil and the economy. He would make a place here. He was seventeen years old; in four years war would break out.

He heard horses now, their hooves striking the hard-packed clay. Immediately he slipped behind a sweet gum and dropped to his stomach. The tree roots pressed hard into him, and he remembered briefly how he and his sister used to play hide-and-seek in the woods behind the house. Within a few minutes a small Federal patrol passed. The men were talking in such low tones he couldn't understand them; then they laughed suddenly. Someone had probably just finished telling some joke or ribald story, he decided. He felt his heart beating fast, but it wasn't pounding as hard as it did before an engagement.

Once they were past, he began moving again. He knew there might be a camp nearby. How many men? he wondered. One company? Two? A regiment? This was what his company and the others with them were supposed to find out. This was why they'd ridden so far east. They'd come farther than he'd wanted. He was tired of riding. His muscles were sore, and he felt them pull now as he walked. He was thirsty too. He hadn't noticed it before the patrol, but he did now. His canteen was back beside his blanket.

He hadn't started out with the cavalry. He'd joined the Eleventh Alabama and had ended up all the way in Virginia. At Seven Pines, on the first day of that battle, in his very first fight, he'd been wounded in the heel. In a little while now, with just a bit more walking, it would begin to hurt, he knew, but not enough to slow him down greatly. He'd spent months in the hospital, where he missed Gaines Mill, Sharpsburg, and Fredericksburg. A long time to heal, but he hadn't lost his foot to the saw, hadn't had to have a piece of himself thrown onto the pile the way a butcher discards unwanted parts of a carcass. Then they'd put him in the cavalry, the Second Alabama, and he'd fought all over Mississippi, North Alabama, Tennessee. They'd been in so many skirmishes and battles that he was now riding his tenth horse, all the others shot out from under him. Each time he'd felt the horse's front legs buckle, and each time there had been that awful pitch forward, over the horse's neck, and every time a prayer that his feet wouldn't tangle in the stirrups and that he wouldn't find himself caught beneath the struggling horse, his leg broken, waiting for some Yankee to shoot him in the head, or worse, in the stomach. That was the only real fear he had, to be gut shot. Those were the wounds that brought the screams. He'd heard them at Seven Pines, and still he was not used to them.

He kept listening for more patrols, but since the one had just passed he doubted there would be another. Still, he was careful. A few more clouds had moved in, and there was less starlight, but a brightness stayed gathered in the road because of the break in the trees. He could find his way as long as he kept the road beside him. He had better cover with the added darkness, if only he remained quiet, which seemed more difficult to do now because somehow the heavier darkness brought with it a silence to the woods, as if the only things that would possibly dare to move in such a place were the "haints" that the slaves believed in. But he didn't believe in haints; he believed only in what he could see and hear and feel, and what he had witnessed these past four years had been, at times, almost too much for his senses: the smell of putrid flesh, the sound of the screams of amputees in the hospital, the itch of his own lice-covered skin.

These were the things he thought of now as he walked, but something quickly called his senses back to the present. Hooves struck the ground in a steady rhythm. He waited and the shadow of a figure broke through the soft light up ahead. For a moment Rafe stood motionless and watched as the man drew closer. Finally he crouched down and leaned against a sweet gum. A messenger probably, he thought. Some Federal officer had more than likely dragged the poor man out of bed and sent him on his way.

The rider came at a slow and steady stride, as if he were simply riding home after a night of hunting or hard drinking. Rafe tried to hug himself closer to the trunk of the tree; and, as he moved, his right boot slipped and scraped across one of the large roots he was standing on. He could feel the bark tearing beneath his weight. The rider suddenly straightened himself in the saddle and pulled on the reins, stopping his horse. He looked slowly toward one side of the road and then the other. Rafe imagined the man's eyes passing the exact spot where he was crouched against the tree. He didn't move; he only thought, I shouldn't have let myself get this close to the road. I should have been more careful.

The man didn't pull his carbine or his revolver, and he didn't call out. He was still several yards ahead. Rafe waited. Perhaps the man was imagining he heard something. It was possible. Many times Rafe had stood picket and thought he heard movement out in the woods. Often it was nothing. The woods at night make you hear things. And even when there was something, usually it was only an owl or some small animal searching for food, a coon or possum or some other scavenger. Maybe the man was deciding that that was all he'd heard.

The rider began to move again now, at the same pace as before. He mumbled softly to his horse, then leaned sideways. Rafe heard the sound of tobacco juice spit between teeth, heard the juice hit the ground. Let him pass, he thought. You don't have to do anything.

Now the rider was even with him. The horse took another step, and Rafe began counting them. In a few seconds the man would be past, the opportunity gone. He was no longer aware now of the pain in his heel, only the quickening of his blood and the tightening of the muscles in his legs and arms and stomach. He counted another drop of the hooves, but he got no further than *three,* the number he and his brothers would count to and then shout when they raced each other as boys. By the time Rafe made the road the rider had just leaned over to spit again, and he caught the man's thick collar in one hand and with the other drove the knife home into the too soft belly.

He kept his arms gripped tight around the man, and the horse reared, broke out from beneath the rider, and ran bucking into the woods. Rafe now held the man in his arms, the knife still

43

buried deep in the man's stomach. He heard him begin to gasp for breath, trying to gather enough air to yell. With his right hand he quickly pulled the knife from the wound, letting the weak body slump to the ground in a sitting position; with his left hand he grabbed the man's chin and pulled up—stretching his neck tight. He made the cut hard and quick, twisting the head as he did so. The blood flowed over his hands like water from a spring, only so much warmer.

He wrapped his arms around the man's chest, still holding the knife, and dragged him from the road and far back into the woods. He dropped him finally and wiped his knife and his hands on the ground and then on his pants, but he could still feel the thin coat of blood that covered his fingers and palms. In the morning he knew he'd see it smeared across his clothes and crusted beneath his fingernails.

He walked slowly back to the edge of the trees, passing the sweet gum where he'd been crouched. He thought of the man and heard him again mumble those soft words to his horse; and Rafe, for the first time, began to form the question that he was afraid he would always be asking himself.

He made another half mile. He knew he was getting close, yet the road didn't look the way he remembered it. Somehow the trees along it looked like a variety he had not seen before. In the daytime everything would surely look the way he remembered. All he had to do tonight was to keep walking. The road would lead him home.

He came to the fork and somehow its angles seemed sharper than he remembered. But he knew he was in the right place. He took the left road, keeping inside the line of the trees.

Another half mile and he took the small lane that wound its way to the left. Up one small rise, and then another, and he came onto open fields that had once been covered by tobacco plants. There was more light out in the open, and he looked for the house. He saw nothing, not a barn even or a single curing shed. Was this the place? He left the road and cut across a fallow field. In the distance, on a small rise where the house was supposed to stand, he saw the three white oaks that grew in the front yard.

He walked slowly. He felt no need to hurry. He made the oaks finally and saw the two piles of bricks that he did not understand at first; each looked somehow foreign, like strange tombs. He realized, after he saw the brick steps between them that led up to nothing, that the piles of brick had been the chimneys. A few timbers lay on the ground. He thought of the countless burned houses he'd ridden past the last year and a half, houses smoldering in the wake of Federal advances. These remains somehow looked no different from the others.

If it hadn't been for the three oaks and the brick steps, he would never have been certain that this was the place he'd run away from. Except for the oaks and the bricks, he felt as if nothing had ever been here, not the house, not the barns and the curing sheds, not the two slave cabins. Perhaps this was why he didn't feel sad now; there was no longer anything to miss, and the absence before him made him feel an absence in the heart.

He took a seat on the steps and looked out across what had been the backyard. He saw the two wells: the one directly behind the house, the one which had been dug when he was twelve—from which the Yankees had probably drawn water for their horses before they burned the buildings; and the other well over to the side of the yard, the one which had gone dry and had once been his refuge.

He hadn't gone right to the well that afternoon. At first he had run across the fields and into the woods not far from the house. He'd found a place there and watched his younger brothers and his sister. They'd stood over the boy, their cousin Ben, who had come to live with them and whom their father had told them to take in as a brother, because that's what he was, their Christian brother, besides being a part of their family. He'd watched as his brothers and sister carried Ben inside, struggling with his long, gangling body, and then came back and called to him in pleading voices and began to search.

At dusk his father came home with his two older brothers and the few slaves they owned. All of them, including the slaves, began to search. He skirted the edges of the fields, staying far enough back in the woods so they wouldn't see him. He then ran toward the house behind the cover of the barns and the curing sheds and made his way to the old well. He'd known that was where he was headed. He let himself down, afraid that the frayed rope would break, and spent eight hours down in that still, damp hole. The darkness, he imagined, was even greater than what the blind lived in; its density impenetrable and frightening in a way he could not have explained. He'd thought of his father often. So many times he'd seen him, one hand holding the razor strop, the other placed upon the Bible while in prayer he asked for guidance in the punishment he was about to bestow. "Let You, O Lord, make me strong and not falter in my duty."

He didn't know what he'd been more worried about after the fight, the condition Ben was in, or the punishment he knew he'd receive. They'd fought before, he and Ben, tussled rather, always more out of sport than anger. That afternoon though, there in the makeshift blacksmith shop under one of the sheds where they'd begun wrestling—mostly out of boredom, although they'd been told to clean up the place—Ben had been getting the best of him for once, and Rafe had begun to cuss, then use his fists. Ben had had to fight back in kind, and he landed two strong blows, one drawing blood from Rafe's nose, the other breaking open his lip. Rafe, not even thinking, had picked up the newly made poker there by the anvil, and the instant he picked it up, he swung, all in one fluid motion. He just missed hitting Ben in the ribs. Rafe could not believe that he'd actually swung the thing, and the look on Ben's face told him that his cousin could not believe it either. But still the two of them stood there, facing each other, the poker in Rafe's hand. It could have ended there in that moment, but as the shock wore off, he felt the heat of his anger rise again, just as the fire rose in the shop when his father worked the bellows while firing a piece of iron. He feinted at Ben and swung the poker again, this time hitting him across his right hip. He lunged then, knocking his cousin to the ground. Once on top, he began pounding him in the side of the head with his fists clasped together, as if together they were the heavy hammer his father used to pound a piece of iron into shape, only his father swung with careful precise blows; he swung in a wild anger. Finally Ben struggled up and began to run, and Rafe picked up a stick of firewood and went after him, stopping him with a hard blow across his back. Once Ben was on the ground again, he stood over him and began to swing the piece of wood down at him, over and over, not aiming and not caring where the blows landed, hardly even aware of what he was doing or how hard he was swinging. Later, as he hid in the woods, shaking, he heard his brothers and sister echo each other with the call "He ain't dead," and he realized the only thing that had saved Ben was that he'd been willing to sacrifice his arms to the blows, and that the bones in each arm must be broken.

He stood up now from the brick steps. He wondered where they all could be, including Ben. Moved into Durham? Fighting in the war? Dead? Perhaps it didn't matter. They were gone; that was all he needed to know. He would not see them again. Maybe there had been no returning to this place he'd left. Then he remembered what he'd done tonight. For a while he'd forgotten it: the run out of the woods, the raising of the knife, and the driving it home. It had been the same kind of fluid movement as when he'd picked up the poker and swung. Had he had to? And that deserter who'd come out of the bushes when he'd stood picket. Had he had to shoot?

He walked over to the near well, lowered and raised the bucket, and drank deeply. He'd forgotten how thirsty he'd been, and the cool water almost made him dizzy. When he was done he let the bucket swing back out over the hole. Because he'd found himself looking at it, he walked over to the old well, leaned against its rotted wooden housing, and looked down. He could see nothing, of course. There was only the same impenetrable darkness, the image he'd lived with that was not an image. He thought of the boy he'd been, the boy who'd hunted and swam with his brothers, and the boy who had crawled up out of that hole. Almost ten years had passed. Something inside him had sent him after Ben that day and had then forced him to have to hide down in the old well, and that same something still remained, it seemed, had perhaps grown into some terrible shape within him, one that he could not describe or see set out before him like the houses and farms he'd seen on the way in.

He began to walk back toward the small lane that had brought him home. There were several miles to cover—and maybe a Federal patrol to dodge. He looked up at the moon. It was lower now, and because of the brightness of the stars beyond it he could just distinguish the outline of its dark half. The best he could judge, he'd make it back to camp right before it disappeared into the tops of the trees.

A Shooting

PHIL ANDERSON wiped the thin layer of sweat from his face with a white handkerchief and looked again out the window from inside the dark of the store. His father-in-law, whom he always called Mr. Wilkie, sat beside him in a cane-bottom chair. Phil had only one lamp burning in the back; and while the front windows usually let in a good deal of light, the day was now overcast. At first he had not lighted more lamps simply because he didn't want the store any hotter than it already was; but now, even though it had grown darker, Dock was out there, striding up and down the street with his face turned toward the store and fixed in a hot stare, and Phil hadn't thought any more about how dim it had grown inside. He mostly kept his gaze trained on Dock, as did Mr. Wilkie, who he knew had good reason for concern.

Phil thought that Dock, because of the way he paced back and forth in the dusty patch of road, looked something like a soldier who was perhaps being punished for an infraction—made to continue his marching until he dropped hot and almost dead in the June heat. He supposed it was also the pistol in the small holster on Dock's belt that gave him his sense of Dock as soldier, but seeing the pistol there was, of course, not unusual.

Upon closer look, though, it seemed to him that maybe Dock didn't really move like a soldier after all. His stride was a little too erratic. There was no measured, military snap in his step. He was pacing more like an angry child who is almost at the point of being told to go and cut his own switch, and no parent would put up with the language coming out of his mouth.

Mr. Wilkie leaned back in his chair and slowly took out his pipe, packed it with tobacco, and lit it after striking a match against the bottom of his shoe. "Are the cattle farmers having trouble with Bangs disease like they were last year?" he asked.

"No. Not right now," Phil said without turning away from the window.

"That's good. It can be tough on a small farmer."

"Yes, sir."

While he spoke and kept watch, Phil somehow continued to eat his lunch of crackers, cheese, and bologna, washing it down with swallows of water from the jar at his feet.

"Reckon what cotton might bring this fall?" Mr. Wilkie asked.

"No telling."

"Still, it looks like a lot of people have planted. They haven't lost faith."

"No, sir."

The louder and more violent Dock's language became, the

softer Mr. Wilkie spoke. His voice was so quiet, so controlled, that if Phil had not known better, it would have seemed to him as if their discussion of local agriculture were taking place in church on the back pew during the middle of a sermon, Dock's voice merely that of the preacher's, outraged and full of hell's fire. But at the end of Dock's tirade, he knew that there would be no final prayer, no gift of redemption offered.

Mr. Wilkie had stepped off the Birmingham train and onto the platform at three o'clock sharp the day before. Phil had taken his hand in a firm and hardy shake and looked him squarely in the eye, and the well-dressed gentleman had responded in like manner, as always. After Phil had retrieved the one bag, Mr. Wilkie asked after family members, especially Phil's father, Rafe. Even though there was some age difference between them—Phil's father being older—the two men were close. They shared a passion for horses. Rafe had served in the cavalry during the War, and Mr. Wilkie, in his younger days, had worked at breaking horses in Arkansas and Texas.

Phil listened to the gravel crunch under their feet as they walked. "We have a new preacher at church," he said, just remembering. "He's a fine one, and we hope you'll come to Sunday service with us."

"Yes, I'd like that," Mr. Wilkie said. "That sounds fine."

Phil inquired then how things were in the shoe business.

When they reached the end of the depot road where it ran into the main street through town, Phil asked if he would like to come up and stay at the store for a while or go on to the house.

"I have a little business to tend to," Mr. Wilkie said.

A Shooting

He had known early on, when his father-in-law began making so many trips down, that it was probably a woman, and a much younger one at that, since Mr. Wilkie had been quiet about it. He was glad for the gentleman. After all, Mr. Wilkie had been a widower for many years, and if a somewhat older man could find companionship, what could be wrong with it? Besides, he'd thought at the time, Mr. Wilkie was seeing his daughter more often on these trips down. But later, when he heard the rumor that Dock might not be the father of the twins his wife had recently lost in childbirth, he could only shake his head. It was just a rumor, but he understood how things were between Dock and his wife, that Dock did not always treat her right. He knew that sometimes she could not leave the house and allow herself to be seen in public. And he knew what a gentle man his father-in-law was.

Mr. Wilkie was late for supper that night.

"What's keeping Father?" Louise said at the table. "And didn't I tell you he'd be late?" She looked at Phil in aggravation.

"Yes, and you were right."

They heard his footsteps then. Phil made ready to rise, and his father pushed back his own chair and wiped his mouth and neatly clipped white goatee with his napkin.

After supper the three men went and sat in the living room. They spoke of the War and of horses. The talk was mostly between the two older men. "My youngest son seems to do all right for himself," Rafe said. "Some fine horses, a fine business, and a fine wife. Not necessarily in that order, of course." The men laughed, but Mr. Wilkie seemed distracted.

At the evening's end, when they stood out on the long porch, Rafe took Mr. Wilkie by the arm. "You'll come to church with us on Sunday, won't you? We've got a fine preacher. Only been here a few weeks. You must hear him."

"I've already told him, Daddy. He says he'll come."

"Good," the father said. The old man started down the steps, then turned back for a moment. "Too bad Dock couldn't have been here tonight," he said. "He's got that wife to look after, though. She's still down in the bed."

Mr. Wilkie was silent. Phil watched his father turn and descend the steps and walk out into the humid night.

Dock was closer now to the store. He walked just past the high wooden porch, quiet for the moment.

Phil swallowed another bite of bologna and hoop cheese. He'd drunk the last of his water, but his mouth was still filled with a greasy taste. It was in his throat too.

"What time your train leave tomorrow?" he said.

"One-fifteen."

Phil heard Dock cough hard and spit on the ground. "I'm sure Louise will put out quite a spread for dinner before you leave." He laughed slightly, as if to say, "There's nothing wrong here."

Then Dock's voice came again, louder, even more violent.

"You say the shoe business has been good lately?"

"Not as good as it could be, but then it never is." Mr. Wilkie took his pipe in his hand and blew out a thin stream of sweet and fragrant smoke that smelled like dried apples.

"No, sir." Phil shook his head, got up, and walked back into the dark part of the store where he poured more water for himself from a jug behind the counter. He swallowed it in several mouthfuls, but the warm water couldn't quite cut through the greasy taste that enveloped his throat. This is senseless, he thought. Why doesn't Dock just get it over with?

Phil looked out front as two young black boys in a wagon filled with sacks of feed rolled past. He recognized one of them as Jeremiah, who often came in the store. They moved slowly at first, but after seeing and hearing Dock, they quickened their team. The only other person Phil could see stood in the doorway of a store across the street. It was a white man. He couldn't tell who.

Things hadn't been like this when his father had come into the store back in the fall and told them what Carl Teclaw had done—how Teclaw had met him in the road, slightly drunk, the both of them on horseback, and how Teclaw had cussed him, called him a tired old man, and told him to get out of his damn way.

"I may be too old to take care of you, Carl," he had said, "but I'll send one of my boys around. You can count on that."

Dock had been furious. "The son of a bitch," he said. "I'm going to kill him."

Phil stepped slowly in front of the door. "No. If he's got to be killed, I'll do it. You're not going to walk in and commit murder, that wouldn't be right."

"Phil is right," the old man said, and with that, the matter was settled, as it always was when their father spoke.

Phil then picked up his .38 caliber pistol, the lemon-squeezer he called it because of the way the safety device was built into the handle, and he and Dock walked together across the street and into Teclaw's store.

"Carl, you've got a pistol here," Phil said. It was more a declaration than a question.

Phil had then taken his white handkerchief from his pocket and let it fall open. "I'll hold one end at arm's length with my right hand. Carl, you hold the other end," he said, describing the way his father had told him duels used to be fought. "Dock will count three and we'll each drop our ends, draw our pistols, and fire."

Teclaw looked down at his feet. "I've got a wife and children. I can't go outside with you."

"I've got a wife at home myself, and a baby boy. Now come on. This has got to be done."

"If I got down on my knees and apologized to your father, would that be enough?"

"All right, Carl," he'd said. "That will satisfy me." He'd hoped then that Dock wouldn't come back later and kill the man on his way home. Their father had taught them better than that, but Dock might do anything.

He knew the shotgun was there behind the counter, not far from where he stood now with the water jug. It was always there, the .12 gauge double-barrel, against the wall, well oiled, loaded with buckshot. His father had given it to him a few years before, at Christmas of '06, if he remembered right. It had kept coming into his mind when he'd been up front with his father-in-law. He did not even have to turn around and look for it in the dim light. He knew exactly where it was. All he had to do was take one step backward and reach. His hand would find it.

He looked up front at Mr. Wilkie. The man was leaning toward the window, and he touched the panes with his finger tips and gently tapped the glass. It was as if he were offering himself as a target, saying, "Go ahead, shoot me through this window." Phil wanted to tell him that he ought to step back. To dare Dock was about as foolish a thing as a man could ever do.

Dock's language was getting worse. *Bastard. Son of a bitch.* These were the words coming out of him now, and if there had ever been a chance that nothing would happen, that Dock would walk away, which wasn't the case, that time had now passed. Mr. Wilkie could not allow it.

Phil stepped away from the counter and toward the back wall. There was no question. None at all. And as he told himself this and reached back for the shotgun, he heard Dock's voice for a moment, not the shouts that were pouring through the open door, but Dock saying, "I did it," his voice trembling, his hands shaking by his sides. And he, Phil, seven years old, had stood behind his older brother feeling the weight of guilt as they both faced their angry father. "I let your horse out of the barn when you told us not to ever go near him," Henry had said—he was still Henry then, had not yet become Dock. He had not even added that it was an accident. He'd just said, "I did it," covering for his younger brother.

Phil picked the shotgun up by the stock, being careful not to get fingerprints on the oiled barrel. He broke open the breach. There was no need to. He knew it was loaded, but he checked anyway, for Mr. Wilkie's sake. He snapped it shut and the metal pieces rang against each other. He knew Mr. Wilkie heard and that the man could not mistake the sound, but he didn't act as if he'd heard, did not turn his head toward the back of the store, did not flinch.

Phil walked then into the stronger light in the front and stood again beside his father-in-law. He leaned down and propped the shotgun beside the window. "If you need it, use it." That was all he said. There was no more talk of diseased cattle or of cotton.

He sat down and then watched as Dock suddenly turned, his eyes squinted, his head tilted. Dock reached for and pulled the pistol from his belt. Mr. Wilkie, in one easy upward and unbroken motion had stood and stepped out the door; he raised the shotgun now as if he were throwing down on a rabbit—a cane-cutter out in the river swamp, maybe. The explosion rang through the store and the smell of sulfur, like sickness, followed. His brother's body was already on the ground. He did not even see it fall. It was just there, sprawled and twisted, Dock's head a red and torn mess. Dirt crusted to his wounds, to his blood-soaked hair.

Phil went behind the counter, reached for his pistol, then walked out onto the porch. Mr. Wilkie stood over the body. A crowd of people had gathered, black and white, the blacks standing farther back. Phil made certain that the crowd saw him there on the porch, saw the pistol in his hand.

Mr. Wilkie looked around at the crowd. He held the shotgun in his right hand, the barrel angled toward the ground. "Has anybody got anything to say about this?" he said. No one spoke or looked at him. "Good. I've got to get back to my business in Birmingham."

Phil watched as his father-in-law walked away with the shotgun. He didn't know if Mr. Wilkie would try to leave that night or the next morning, or if he would go and talk with the sheriff. But he was sure of one thing, his father-in-law would face the old man before he left. He would say, "I'm sorry. I had to kill your son."

He stepped back into the store, found a cloth sack, and took it outside. People were still gathered around the body, and he walked between them and spread the sack over his brother's face, making sure that it also covered the thick dark pool beside his head. He stood there then, looking down at the body that had grown solid in the middle. When did that happen? he wondered. When did he become so heavy-set? He was no longer aware of the people around him. For a moment he could not think what to do next, and in that instant felt like a boy bewildered by the strange and unfathomable ways of things that a father tries to make him understand.

He began walking toward the old house where he and Henry had grown up. As soon as he made the turn in the road, he would see it. The wide porch, the dog trot. He walked slowly. The sun had come out again and sweat ran down his face. It ran into the corners of his mouth, and he tasted its salt on his tongue. At the turn, he stopped, stepped down into the shallow ditch beside the road, and bent over, holding one hand against his stomach. His throat burned, and he waited on what he'd eaten. Afterward he took out his white handkerchief and cleaned the corners of his mouth; he stepped then out of the ditch and continued.

The funeral can't be tomorrow, he thought. There would be regular Sunday service. He and Louise would go, of course, unless he was needed to sit with the body. And besides, tomorrow would be too soon for a funeral. Family had to be notified.

He was almost to the house now, walking slowly, but steadily. He could see his father sitting in a chair just inside the dog trot; then the old man rose. He knew his father had heard the shot, that he might even somehow know what had happened. But he would have to tell him. He would have to say, "I handed him the gun." He had no fear of what his father would say. The old man would understand. He had done what he knew was right, what his father had taught him.

He approached the steps, his throat still burning.

Conjure Woman

"I T'S ALL FOOLISHNESS," she told him when he mentioned
what had been in his mind. They were standing there in the
hall, just come in from church. She still had her hat on, the blue
one, and was taking off her gloves, holding her Bible under one
arm as she did so. "Foolishness," she said again, the pitch of
her voice rising. Conrad had heard her irritation many times
before, that high tone, and could only wonder now if May was
even more angry than she wanted him to know. It was hard to
tell with her.

They'd been married only two years ago, November 5, 1930.
Sometimes he still had a difficult time understanding her. But
she was a good woman. He knew that. Didn't she often visit with
whoever was on the prayer list if they were sick and take food to
their families? He knew she didn't do it out of any sense of duty
either; it was because she wanted to do it, because it made her

feel good. She worked in the store, too, whenever he needed her. And at the end of that first year, when it looked like he wasn't going to make it in the store, she'd stood behind him, told him that if the business failed it would *not* be his fault. He'd worked hard. She could have blamed him. She didn't.

"Foolishness," she'd said. Well, he had his doubts about it too, but he didn't really see any *harm* in going down to see the old black woman. Maybe she *could* tell him something about who had broken into his store a week ago Saturday night. Or had it been early on Sunday morning? Maybe she could tell him at least that much. Maybe.

It was Bragg's idea. He would never have thought of going to talk to the old woman himself. He hardly knew her since she rarely came into the store. But Bragg, his boyhood friend, and now sometime employee when he was needed and sober, had brought up the idea, as if going to talk to an old conjure woman who lived down on the Black Fork was the thing everybody did when something was stolen from them, or when they needed answers to problems. It was like Bragg to come up with a thing like this. Just like him.

"You know how they are," Bragg had said. "They all believe that stuff. Niggers do. Hoodoo, you know. Maybe there's a little something to it. I ain't saying there is for sure, but you can't tell. They live different from us. Maybe they know about things that we don't."

"You really believe that?"

Bragg only smiled.

Conrad had heard tell of how she could see things that had happened or would soon happen. And he'd heard, years ago, how she hoodooed old Isaiah Williams, who lived over on the

Caulfield place. He'd been bad-mouthing her for some reason or another, the story went. Not behind her back, but right to her face. Cussed her, too. She struck a match while he was running on there in front of her, struck it as if she were going to light her pipe, but instead took the match, still burning orange flame, and without him even realizing what she was doing until it was too late, stuck it into his wide open mouth and against his tongue. Months later, the cancer came on him. It pulled his mouth, or what was left of it, into a terrible pink-gum grimace. "Hoodooed," all the blacks said. "He been hoodooed." May knew the story too.

"All right," Conrad had said. "I'll go." But even as he spoke, he knew somehow that May would not want this, that she would feel such an aversion to the idea that he would have to hear that high tone in her voice. Or she might try to dismiss the idea in that silent way she had—look up toward the ceiling, close her eyes, grit her teeth, and shake her head, as if to say, "Why must you aggravate me so?"

But he saw now, standing there in the hall, that silence would not be her tactic. "It's just not the right thing to do," she said evenly. She clutched her Bible tightly to her bosom and looked down at it. It was not the new Bible he had given her, the nice red leather one she could carry to church with pride, but her old one with the frayed black covers that was filled with marks and notes in pencil. He knew how she studied it, how she quietly tried to live her life by its dictates.

"Why is it wrong to just go and talk to the old woman?" he said.

With her free hand she removed her hat. "Because the Bible says it's wrong." With this she walked out of the hall and into their room. The floor shook with each step. The sound of heel against wood rang out like the sharp report of a gun.

Something hadn't felt right when he'd first walked into the store, he just hadn't known what. They'd gone to church that morning of course, then eaten dinner, and he had taken a nap afterward. She'd joined him, as she only occasionally did, and when he awoke and pulled her close, she, though silent as always, opened herself to him.

That was the one sweet memory he had of that day. The others were not as pleasant. Late in the afternoon he'd decided to take care of a little book work. He never opened on Sunday, but half an hour of adding figures in the quiet, empty store was all right, acceptable. May had even gone with him, said she needed a few things.

The air. That's what it was, the thing that hadn't felt right. He'd unlocked the door, pushed it open, and noticed that a faint sweet scent of honeysuckle hung inside. But how could that be? The store was closed up tight. He dropped his keys into his pocket. May followed him in. He walked toward the side counter where the register sat and noticed suddenly the sunlight that broke hard across the meat counter in back.

"Look," he said, as a sick feeling filled his stomach.

The side door stood wide open. He passed quickly behind the counter where the salted meat lay, hoping that somehow he'd left the door open, but he saw the hasp broken and the other lock pried out, the wood around it splintered. He pushed the screen door open, as if whoever had done this might still be out there with a crowbar in his hand. He noticed then the torn screen wire. There was nothing out there of course, except

honeysuckle growing along the close barbed-wire fence. He
stood staring for a moment. He took a deep breath that he
hoped would calm him before he had to turn around and take
stock of what had been stolen. In that breath he detected not
just the sweet odor of honeysuckle, but a hint of something
bitter and wild, hardly noticeable, but strong enough to in-
crease his nausea. Then he noticed the footprints in the dirt, as
clear as if they'd been left on purpose.

He turned to face May. Her jaw was tight, and in the slant of
light from the door he could see how her eyes were squinted,
narrowed, as if she were trying to hold in the anger behind
them; but the glare there was unmistakable. "Let's see what's
been taken," he said. She turned mechanically and picked up a
pencil and pad of paper off the counter.

He knew what would probably be missing: cigarettes, shotgun
shells, knives, an assortment of pants and shirts. Conrad called
out the missing items as best he remembered. May wrote them
down, working in silence, listing each in her neat and even hand.
The only sound she made was the scratch of pencil against paper.
After almost half an hour of work, when they were about finished, she finally spoke. "We must be thankful, Conrad."

"Thankful?" he said, utterly bewildered by what he'd just
heard.

"Yes, thankful. At least we don't keep money here. At least
that. It could be worse."

She seemed already resigned to it. That suddenly. He could
hear it in the low flat tone of her voice, but couldn't believe it.
Sometimes he simply could not understand her.

He turned from her and looked at the table where he kept
shoes and work boots. They all seemed to be in place. He

remembered the footprints outside in the dirt, and then an idea came to him. He could learn something at least about who it was, or maybe how many there had been. He picked up several pairs of shoes, carried them with him toward the door, and stepped outside.

"What are you doing?" May called out after him.

He didn't answer. He kneeled down in the dirt and carefully placed the different-sized shoes in each print until he found a fit. Nine. All size nine. That meant probably one man, small in build.

Then something caught his eye. The head of a hammer lay in the dirt not far from the prints. It must have broken off when he pried the hasp loose, Conrad thought. He picked it up and noticed that a piece of the right claw was broken. It reminded him of a chipped tooth somehow. He held the rusted piece of metal tight in his hand, his grip hardening as he imagined the man who had done this.

May walked to the door. "You'll have to drive and get the sheriff," she said in her calm and reasonable manner.

"Yes," he said. "I know."

That evening the sheriff came. The man didn't do anything more than Conrad had done earlier, just walked around, looked things over. "Could have been anybody," he said.

Conrad could see where the river wound its way by the break in the trees up ahead. Even above the smell of the cedars that grew so thick he could smell the river, the Black Fork. It was not exactly a clean smell; there was the slight odor of mud and fish in it, but still it was good, pungent, something you wanted to breathe in deep. There was nothing bitter about it.

He hadn't told May that he had decided to go today. She knew well enough that he was going sometime soon, but he figured that she didn't need to know the exact time and day. It would be easier on him if she didn't.

He saw the house now through the trees, but just barely. Then a flash of red, and when it stopped, Conrad, moving closer, made out the figure of a black woman. He walked past the cedars and into the clean-swept dirt yard. She was standing over a pump, a bucket in her hand. A bandana, red with white designs, was tied tightly around her head. Not a hair showed beneath it. She stopped pumping the handle and looked suddenly at him; a kind of quiet came across her features, a hardness in her face muscles.

"She in the house," the woman said.

"How do you know who I want to see?" he asked.

"All the white folks come see Mama."

He followed her while she called out to her mother. The wooden porch sagged a bit, but the house itself stood straight enough. It was unpainted, the boards a kind of bone-gray color, but well kept. No rotten shutters. The tin roof even looked fairly new; it wasn't turned deep red with rust like so many of them.

Ain't a bad little place, he thought. Not bad at all.

Conrad guessed he'd been expecting the most run-down shack he'd ever want to see, some dark-looking place with no windows and with maybe a big black pot outside for boiling roots and herbs for potions and such. But there was only an old washtub, a basket of clothes beside it.

By the time he was up to the porch steps an old black woman, a little stooped but still able to move with some ease, walked onto the porch. She gave her daughter a look, and the girl quickly went into the house.

"Good evening, Mr. Conrad," she said. Conrad did not act surprised that she knew who he was, or even at the fact that she seemed to have expected him. She motioned to the chair on the porch. "Please set down," she said. He did, and she sat in a swing across from him and waited, it seemed, for him to begin. He hesitated, feeling suddenly as if this were a foolish thing.

"Can I helps you with something?" Her manner and tone made it clear to Conrad that she was used to visits like this.

"It's about my store being broken into. I want to know if you can tell me something about who it was that did it."

She nodded her head. "Just tell me what you know," she said, "and don't leave nothing out. Not the smallest littlest thing."

He told her about the honeysuckle smell, the door being broken open, even about the light across the counter; then told her about the piece of hammer and the footprints, only he didn't say anything about measuring the prints; that was one detail he left out. "Don't ever tell all you know," he'd often said to Bragg. "Always hold a little back."

"Does you have that piece of hammer with you?"

He reached into his deep weighted pocket and handed it to her. She took it, ran her fingers over the chipped place in the metal, then cupped her hands around it as if it were some kind of precious stone.

While he'd been telling her the details of what he'd found in the store that Sunday, she'd listened like a child might listen to a grown-up tell a story or to a preacher telling a simple parable. Before he came he'd half expected her to shut her eyes and rock back and forth in some kind of crazy trance, but she just sat there, looking at him with large, wide open, blank brown eyes, as if she were looking at a picture or maybe a barge going down the river. Maybe she did see a picture in her mind, he thought. A picture of the man.

Now, while she held the hammer in her hands she closed her eyes every so often and gently pushed herself in the swing with the tip of her toe. Her eyes opened and shut in a rhythm that equaled the rocking motion of the swing. Still, there was nothing trance-like about it. She looked more like she was drifting off for a short nap. There was no hypnotic humming or moaning emanating from her as he'd half expected. She only cleared her throat once or twice.

Finally she leaned over and handed Conrad the piece of metal, and as she did he smelled first a sweet scent, like baby powder on her skin, then detected a sharp whiskey odor on her breath.

"He a white man," she said. "Ain't from around here, though. I knows that."

"What size man is he?" Conrad said.

"He small. Mean, too. He do this kind a thing right regular. He sorry. Sorry trash."

"Where's he from?" Conrad said.

"Live across the river somewhere."

"Which one? The Tennahpush or Black Fork?"

"Don't know. Can't see it good. Just see a little old white house. Ain't no woman there."

"You can tell all that from a hammer?" he said.

She didn't answer. Hardly seemed to have heard him. She turned her head and spat past the porch's edge, then slowly faced him again, wiping her bottom lip with the back of her dark hand.

"What'd he do with what he took?" Conrad said.

"It done been got rid of. It gone."

"I got one more question," he said. "What size shoe does he wear?"

She studied him, looked at his face and, oddly enough, at his feet, then leaned back. "Nine," she announced.

"Well all right then," Conrad said and stood to leave. He reached into his pocket, pulled out two dollars, and handed them to the woman. "Reckon you got something you can spend some of this on?" he said, not too loudly, as if there were a secret between them. "Something you might soon run out of? Maybe need a refill?" He smiled.

She took the two bills, folded them carefully, stuck them into her deep bosom, and said, "Thank you, sir. Come back. I helps when I can. White or black."

He descended the steps and, looking back, saw that she was already leaning far back in the gently rocking swing, almost asleep.

When he returned to the store, Conrad found Bragg sitting in his usual place, a cane-bottom chair near the door. He was drinking a dope, and there were already two empty bottles on the floor beside him. When he saw Conrad, Bragg's face filled with anticipation, like a boy being handed a present wrapped in shining paper.

"Well, what about it?" Bragg said.

First he told George—the black man who worked part-time for him—that he could go on home since things were quiet, that Bragg would stay until closing. The black man stopped straightening the buckets of lard. "Yes, sir," he said.

So he told Bragg what happened. Told him everything the old woman said and did: how she said to tell her all the details, not to leave anything out, how she held the hammer and rocked herself in the swing, and how she described the man.

"That ain't much of a story, Conrad," he said when Conrad was finished.

"But she knew the size shoe," Conrad said. "She got it right."

"Yeah, she did. But still. I figured there would be a lot more to her."

"What do you mean?"

"I don't know. I wanted to hear about some of those nigger doings. She didn't chant or carry on or nothing?" he said and shook his head sadly. Conrad could see the disappointment on his face.

By the end of the evening, at closing time, Conrad knew what a mistake he'd made in saying anything at all to Bragg. When someone white came into the store, Bragg had announced, "Conrad been down to see that hoodoo woman," and then he'd launched into an exaggerated account of his visit. He didn't tell things the same way twice, and none of what he said sounded anything like what happened. Bragg had her in trances and shouting and swallowing strange mixtures to bring the trance states on. Conrad just shook his head. He'd let Bragg go on with it each time.

"It just wasn't much of a story the way you told it," Bragg said as a sort of apology after he'd given the third account of it to a salesman.

May walked in right before closing, gently easing the screen door shut behind her. "Hello, Bragg," she said.

Bragg started up. Conrad shook his head again, walked to

the back, but finally came up front again. When he did he could tell that this particular version was the wildest one yet, as if Bragg had just been warming up with the others. "Conrad said she chewed on some kind of a root," Bragg was saying. "Then she gets the shakes and starts dancing around the porch, hollering something crazy. And this mean daughter of hers what's wearing a red turban on her head comes out the house and tries to take the piece of root from her, but the old woman jerks it away. It must have been a sight. They started scuffling right there on the porch. Conrad said he didn't know what to think."

May, standing in the middle of the floor between the counter that Conrad now stood behind and the circle of chairs where Bragg sat, looked at Conrad with an expression that went beyond exasperation, as if Conrad were telling the story and not Bragg. She was angry, but he knew that she would try to hide it, would hold her anger in this time.

"I have come for vanilla extract," she announced. She smoothed the front of her skirt and walked to the shelf.

Conrad saw that Bragg was not deterred by her cool display, had not really noticed it.

"She about told Conrad who it was," Bragg said.

"That ain't so," Conrad finally broke in. "She just described him as best she could. I don't know who it is."

"If she'd known him, she could of told you his name. She could see him in her mind I bet—what's left of it." Bragg laughed. "That root done took most of it away. She didn't know him to call him by name. That's all. She must have been something once she got on that wild root. Conrad said it could make her see the past and the future. Said it could make her see God and the devil too. I believe it must have brought loose the devil in her. That's what it did. Brought out the devil. Conrad said her eyes even turned red."

"Hush, Bragg," she said through her teeth. "That root has nothing to do with anything. The devil she has in her is the one she let in when she started practicing all that foolishness." Although her words seemed to be directed at Bragg, she was staring again at Conrad. He saw how her eyes were narrowed, like on that Sunday when they'd walked into the store and saw the side door open. Her hands were tightly clenched into fists at her sides now. There was suddenly something almost frightening about her. He knew how angry she must be, how angry she must have really been when he first spoke to her about the old woman. But he didn't know, could not understand, what it was exactly that made her so angry.

Conrad and May sat directly across from each other at the small table in the kitchen that night. There was still a little light left outside, but not enough for them to see well, so May lit the coal-oil lamp, but kept it turned low. Conrad wished she hadn't lit it. He didn't want to have to see her face so clearly. He knew she was still angry from the silence she kept. Luckily she kept her face turned down toward her plate. He watched her fork disappear into her mouth time after time.

"Kind of a slow day," he said, testing her. She said nothing, only cut a slice of tomato in half.

"Tomatoes are good," he said.

Again, nothing.

"So you ain't going to talk, huh? I expected you wouldn't. I don't see why you're so mad about it. Going down there didn't hurt nothing. She's just an old nigger woman. Some people are scared of her I know, but I ain't. Don't you be bothered about her."

"I'm not."

"Look, all that stuff Bragg said, he made it up. She only asked me some questions, wanted to hold the head of the hammer I found. Then she described him. Said he was white and built small. Said he wasn't married and lived somewhere across the river—that he wasn't from around here."

"That could be anybody," she said. "She didn't tell you anything."

"But she did."

"What?"

"I asked her his shoe size, and she told me, May. Told me exactly right. Now how could she of done that if it wasn't something to her? I'm going to ask the sheriff if it sounds like anybody he knows of."

"Conrad," she said, her voice rising, "you mean you really believe that mess?"

"How else could she of known?"

"Don't you sit here in my kitchen and tell me you believe what some old heathen nigra woman says. Don't you do it! It's not right, all that mess. It's evil." She was standing now, pointing her finger at him and shaking it as if it were some kind of a weapon, a knife maybe or even a pistol. The light from the lamp lit her face with a yellow glow, and her eyes shone more brightly than the lamp that illuminated them. They had a kind of wet glare in them that made him look away.

"You let me eat my supper in peace, damnit," he said. "Go sit out on the porch or something. I've had enough of this. Leathy Ann can take up these dishes in the morning."

She turned then. He did not watch her; he simply heard her steps as she walked out of the kitchen and onto the back porch.

He continued to sit there in the dim light from the lamp. He bit into a cold biscuit. It had gotten wet, and the dough stuck in his mouth like a cold lump of clay.

On Saturday night, the busiest time of the week, the store was crowded with the throng of people, mostly black, who pushed their way in from the street, up and down the aisles, and finally to the two tables in the back corner where blacks could socialize. The one table in front was reserved for whites.

The street outside and the few stores along it were always so crowded on Saturday nights that it would be hard for an outsider to believe that so many people lived in and around Riverfield, or that they would all be gathered in such a way for anything less than a carnival. But then, maybe this Saturday night ritual, this gathered mob, was a kind of carnival in and of itself. Conrad kept late hours because of the extra business, and he also kept, stuck in his belt and under his shirt, a .38 caliber pistol that had belonged to his father. There were often fights and cuttings out on the street, at least one every Saturday night. If any trouble came inside, which it sometimes did, he wanted always to be ready. And tonight May was working. Bragg had come in drunk, too drunk to be of any help.

Conrad, in the middle of boxing groceries, watched May as she rang up a sale. He could see from her expression that she was tired, but as she turned to face a new customer, black, she smiled, said, "Good evening." George, not far from her, was working steadily at gathering items as they were called out to him.

It was half-past-eleven when Conrad noticed the crowd of

blacks suddenly part way down one aisle, and he saw the con-jure woman. They parted for her the way they would for no one else. It wasn't only fear, Conrad sensed, but out of respect that they made room for her.

He watched her make her way toward the back and then lost sight of her as the crowd closed behind. He turned quickly toward May, to see if she had seen, but May, he remembered, would not recognize the old woman, did not really know her at all. May was still ringing up sales, aware of nothing unusual. What did it matter if the old woman came in? Conrad thought. She'd been in a few times before. He turned and waited on a customer, sold some Tube Rose snuff, some Prince Albert, and some papers. Later someone wanted rag bologna, and he pushed his way back to the meat counter in the corner opposite the tables.

He was slicing what he hoped was a pound of sausage when he heard the scream. It was low and guttural, but unmistakably belonged to a woman. He dropped the butcher knife, and his hand went automatically to his belt. He didn't bring the gun out, just made sure that it was there. The first person he saw as he turned toward the scream was the conjure woman. She was standing at the end of the counter. "I wants me some sausage too," she said.

He didn't answer, but made the few quick steps toward the tables, where the scream had come from. The crowd moved for him the way it had for the conjure woman. He looked down and saw Viola, a large old black woman who had traded with him since he opened, crouched over holding her stomach. A knife lay on the floor at her feet, and blood ran down her leg and onto the crushed heel of her worn shoe. With help he stretched her out on the bench, and someone handed him a clean towel from behind the counter. He pressed it across the long cut that had opened up her dress and her dark flesh.

"Somebody go get Dr. Hannah," he said. He looked at Viola. "Who did this?"

"I don't know," she said. "It too crowded. I didn't see."

With his free hand he picked up the knife from the floor and wiped the blood off on the edge of the towel. Its blade was about four inches long. It was sharp. He could see that well enough. Someone had honed it carefully. But the handle was the thing that struck him most. It was a rudely but intricately carved piece of wood and on one side of it was the figure of a large woman. Revenge, he decided.

He looked around at the faces. No one's expression told him anything. Never give themselves away. Never. He noticed that the conjure woman was gone. But then it couldn't have been her. It was not possible, he thought. She'd been already standing at the counter when he heard the scream. She couldn't have moved that fast.

"Viola cussed that conjure woman's daughter other day," someone said. "Cussed her bad."

"That what somebody told me," another said.

"Conjure woman must a did it."

Conrad didn't speak. The next face he saw was May's. She looked at him accusingly, as if he had been responsible for what had happened, as if he had brought the conjure woman into the store and handed her the knife, the knife that could never even have been in her hand.

May walked up close to him. Surprisingly she took the knife from him, and after a moment looked curiously at the handle.

"She didn't do it, May. She was too far from Viola. I saw that much."

May didn't answer with words at first. Her expression and her narrowed eyes said loudly enough *That woman did it. She is an evil thing. I told you not to see her.* And then, aloud: "Hoodoo doesn't work, but then it doesn't have to, not when she's got this." She waved the knife. "Cut someone. Burn their mouth. It doesn't matter to her."

Sunday morning May took her worn Bible to church, clutching it tightly to her as they walked the short distance without speaking. All morning she had been silent, as she had the night before after coming home. In bed he had crawled close to her and put his arms around her, gently, but she'd pushed him away. He didn't even try to speak to her now. It was no use, he knew. Eventually she would come out of it. This is the way she always did. Still, she was a good woman. He knew that. Hadn't she worked hard Saturday night?

After church they had a quiet dinner at the small table in the kitchen. Later he took a nap, or at least tried to; she remained in the living room. Finally he rose and told her that he was going up to the store to do a little book work. She nodded, said, "All right." Mostly he was going to get away from her for a while, and he knew that she realized this.

All the way to the store he half worried that he would open the door and smell honeysuckle, see the slant of light through the side door, and find more merchandise gone. But he opened the door to a dark and hot store, and he was thankful.

He added a few charge tickets and filed them. That was really all there was to do. Mostly he sat and thought about May, trying to understand why she always became more and more silent the angrier she got. It was as if some instrument inside her measured her anger and at a certain point tripped a mechanism that shut her off, held her anger inside. What did that? Why? Was she afraid of something?

He closed the ticket cabinet with a firm slam, walked out of the store, locked the door behind him, and walked home, anticipating an evening filled with more silence.

As he passed Dr. Hannah's house, he heard the shouting. "I've told you to get out of here! Now go on!" The voice was not one he recognized. Then he was able to look over his fence, also covered with honeysuckle, and through the small stand of oaks in his front yard. May stood in the frame of the open door. "Get away," he heard her say again—saw her say it this time. Then she ran back into the house, and he came on toward the gate, walking fast.

She was there standing at the door, the conjure woman. One foot inside the house, the other still outside on the porch. "All I wants is to talk with Mr. Conrad," she said. Her voice was loud. "Sees can he loan me two dollars till Saturday. I know he here."

Before Conrad could speak he saw her take another step so that she was no longer standing on the porch at all, but was inside the house, swaying suddenly, grabbing for the door frame and falling backward, then catching herself before she fell. "Drunk," he whispered to himself. "Drunker than Bragg last night." By the time he opened the gate, May was again at the door, standing partially behind it and trying to close out the dark staggering figure. The conjure woman pushed, or fell, he couldn't tell which, against the wide oak door, swinging it completely open as she shouted.

"I wants to see . . ."

"I told you, you evil black thing, that Mr. Conrad's not here!" She then raised the pistol, the one with a pearl handle that he had given her, and she saw him, Conrad, at the instant when the pistol was aimed straight at the black woman's head. But May didn't stop when she saw him, didn't let the gun down. It was as if she had gone too far to back away, he thought, could not stop whatever force had been released and put in motion. No matter that her husband was here and could make the woman go away. It seemed to Conrad that the mechanism that held her in check had malfunctioned. He was shocked, felt a kind of fear even, when he saw the intensity and the manner in which her anger—or whatever one might call it—manifested itself. He could see a man, some men, anyway, in other situations perhaps, acting in this way. Even some women, but not May. He had thought something like this beyond her, thought that she hadn't the capacity for it.

He was almost to the steps now. "May!" he called. The black woman turned toward him, came down off the steps, almost stumbling. Then he was on the steps himself, having passed the black woman, and now stood between the two of them. He wanted to say *Are you crazy, May?* but stopped himself, or rather she stopped him with a look in her eyes that went beyond fierceness. It seemed that she had lost her awareness of him. Her eyes were trained only on the conjure woman. "Evil," May had called her. Well, maybe not evil, something close to it, he thought, but as he thought it he wasn't looking at the old black woman, but at May, or at least at that part of her that he had never seen before.

He stepped onto the porch and to the door, reached out, and

took the pistol from May's hand. He had to pry her fingers loose before she would relinquish it. "Go back inside and sit down," he said.

She turned to him. "Get that nigger out of here," she said, pushing the words through her teeth, like venom. Sweat ran down her face, darkened the edges of her hair.

"Go inside," he said. He took hold of her, turned her toward the door. The sweat on the back of her neck had soaked the top of her dress, and the hard acrid scent that came from her body stung his nose.

She strode into the house, and he shut the door behind her. He came down the steps, reached into his pocket, and handed the old woman two dollars. "Don't come back," he said.

"No, sir," she said. "I won'ts. I thanks you."

He found her inside the kitchen, sitting partially slumped in a chair before the little table. The coal-oil lamp was lit and made a yellow light in the room. Outside, shadows were gathered against the windows.

"What happened out there?" he said.

"I don't know."

"You were afraid of her?"

"Yes. Afraid."

"That she might have a knife?"

"Yes. No. I don't know."

"And now?"

"Still afraid."

"But of what? She's gone and I'm here now."

"Yes, I know."

"And you're still afraid?"

"Yes," she said, "but not of the old woman." She would not face him. He wondered if she felt a kind of shame. He did not say anything else, just looked at her—at the way she held her head down, saw the way a shadow covered her face like a veil. He remembered briefly when they were first married, remembered being pleased with what a good woman he had.

He moved a chair up next to her, sat down, and pulled her toward him.

A Visitor Home

AS CAROLINE REED sorted through her mail, standing in front of the taut screen-wire partition above the wooden counter in the Riverfield post office, she almost missed the letter. It came up immediately after the Episcopal Church newsbulletin and just before the monthly bill for the post office box—both of which came in larger envelopes. But when she did finally spot the letter she recognized the handwriting even before she saw the return address; the cramped, careful script released some small emotion in her that she couldn't quite identify. She hadn't expected the letter. At the same time she wasn't surprised. Hamilton wrote every few years, if only to let her know that he was still alive. The tone of his letters was always sad; if she had tried to think of an actual sound, they might have carried the diminishing toll of the Episcopal church bell, ringing the Sabbath each Sunday over Riverfield. But the tone of her brother's letters never affected her very deeply. She knew that Hamilton understood why things were the way they were, why he couldn't come home.

She didn't open the envelope immediately. She shuffled slowly through the remainder of the mail, her thin fingers picking methodically over each piece; then she walked slowly outside and across the road. She had always been thin—her arms long and spare, her legs spindly—but lately her slightness seemed somehow exaggerated by her sixty years, the two conditions acting together to create someone she didn't feel she completely recognized each morning as she combed her hair in front of the bathroom mirror and studied the lined reflection.

Despite her age, she continued to dress in a fashion that she believed made people take notice. She had always worn bright colors and accessories—scarves, hats, and long shawls that she draped around herself in a manner clearly her own. The garments she wore were ordinary pieces of clothing, and she knew that anyone observing them closely would see that each piece was in less than excellent condition; but with the pieces woven into a pattern of her own, she felt they somehow lost their ordinary, even shabby, look. And she felt the same way about the formal manner in which she carried herself, the air with which she moved—that it made her appearance different, refined.

She sat carefully down on the shaded red bench beneath the awning of Anderson's store and tore the envelope open. The letter was brief. She scanned it quickly, her dark glance moving across the cream-colored page. As she read Hamilton's small script, the unnamed emotion she had experienced earlier began to firm and define itself, focusing eventually into full-fledged anger. She read through the letter a second time, neatly folded it, and gathered the other pieces of mail together, then stood and started with short, determined steps toward the small house behind the store. She would tell Aiken.

Even though her younger brother lived with her, and was cared for by her, she knew he despised her. It was only out of necessity that they occupied the same house; the reasons were financial, the arrangement mostly because Aiken was the way he was. His entire life had been spent in the wheelchair, the chair he could not even propel. Except for a few fingers on his right hand, he could move only from the neck up. But if someone were persuaded to open a Coke for him at the store, and to put the slender neck of the bottle into his mouth, he would clench it with his large teeth and drink the entire contents, raising and lowering it as he gulped. And he could travel. His wheelchair fit into a specially made cart that he called his chariot. Satan, his pony, pulled it, and while the animal had often lived up to its name before Aiken acquired him, with the leather reins tied together and looped around his neck, Aiken could pull on either of the straps with his teeth and handle the pony as expertly as a jockey.

Caroline knew that Aiken's feelings about her weren't very different from those he had about most other people; they were only more intense. It had something to do with the amount of brandy she drank, and perhaps the number of men she used to see. Several years earlier she had bent too near his chair to pick up a shattered glass, and Aiken had bitten her on the right buttock, clamping his teeth through her thin dress into the soft flesh there and hanging on like a snapping turtle until he'd drawn blood. There had been that other incident, too, when he'd somehow gotten ahold of her pistol and pointed it at her, but she had managed to take it from him. The scene wasn't something she liked to recall.

She walked now past the ancient oak that threw its shadow over the buildings like the shadow of time itself and picked her way to the house through the dead limbs scattered on the yard. Some of the limbs lay caught on the rusted tin roof of the house, as though someone had placed them there in some hopeless attempt to conceal the structure.

The house itself was small. At its front a plywood ramp led from the packed dirt of the yard directly to the unpainted pine door. Beside the ramp sat the chair in which Caroline read. Occasionally a small, curly-haired boy named Peter Finley would come by, and she would read to him about her family from her dog-eared copy of *Stars Fell on Alabama*.

Inside the house were a sitting room with worn furniture, a bedroom, and at the back a tiny makeshift kitchen with a hand pump over the sink. Jutting from the side of the house, from Caroline's bedroom, stood another room that had been hurriedly built of studs and plywood, and covered with green roofing paper. Its ceiling hovered only five feet above the floor and made the space look more like a child's playhouse than part of an actual dwelling. But the height of the room made little difference since it belonged to Aiken. Overall, the house looked as if it belonged in Jackson Quarter, like one of the many owned by the black families there. But Caroline moved about the tiny rooms as if she were in any one of the better homes that were parceled around Riverfield.

She knew a great deal about the finer homes. Her family had built the finest house in all of West Alabama, complete with

86

columns, marble mantels, stables, and servants. There had been slaves there long ago. She'd spent her childhood and most of her adult life in that house, but twelve years earlier, in 1948, she'd had to sell it. Now it was listed on the state historical register, often opened for pilgrimages.

But Caroline knew that despite the many occupants in the old home, she and her brothers and her parents had been the last people who had known *how* to live there. She carried that knowledge with her now through the small rooms.

Aiken was sitting outside the house just within the shadow of the back porch when Caroline looked out the kitchen window and saw him. She opened the door and walked down the two wooden steps. His body seemed lifeless in the chair, but his thick face was full of vigor. Beside him, on the ground in front of a lawnmower, sat a black youth.

"Which screw you say, Mr. Aiken?" the youth was asking.

"Which one did I just get through telling you?"

"You say the long one."

"Then why'd you ask me? Just take that long one and put the airfilter . . . No! No! The airfilter. Yes, that!"

Caroline stood near the boy now. "What you doing, Aiken?"

"What's it look like? I'm putting this lawnmower back together," he said, as if actually doing the work himself.

"Aiken, I've got a letter here," Caroline said.

"So."

"I mean we've got a letter we need to talk about. You best send Isaac away now."

Aiken looked at the boy, waiting to see if he would leave of his own accord, but he remained sitting, his nimble fingers lying still on top of the engine, waiting.

87

"Well, you heard her," Aiken finally said. "You better go get into trouble somewhere else."

The boy ambled away toward the store, and Caroline thrust the letter in front of Aiken. "Hamilton says he wants to come home. And this time he's not asking just to come for a visit."

"So the thief wants to come home? Return to the scene of the crime? Does he think we'll forgive him?"

"Hush. There's no use in saying such things. He says he's going to come up at the end of the week to look things over."

Caroline didn't prepare for Hamilton's coming. She told no one. She hoped that he would never arrive, though she knew he would. By the end of the week she began to take the dark bottle more and more often from the kitchen shelf and so had to hear more and more of Aiken's tirades. But the larger the portion she drank, the better it blunted his words.

On Friday, Caroline sat in one of the worn chairs in the front room and looked up when something blocked the light from the screen door. She stood up slowly, opened the door, and said a stiff hello, then found herself a little surprised that she felt glad to see her brother finally standing before her in the flesh. He was tall, his hair thin and mostly gray, his face lined and sagging. In his features she slowly recognized something of her own, something she had felt she no longer saw in the mirror in the mornings.

And then she suddenly saw him as he had been years earlier, standing in the side doorway of the house wearing dirty clothes, looking in, saying, "Come on, Sister. If you're going to go fish off the dam with me, you better get your boots on and hurry." And she had hurried.

She moved back from the door now and took a breath.

"Come in," she said, forcing a sharp tone.

He entered the room, taking small steps, and looked from side to side.

"Thank you, Sister," he said. "I was hoping I might hear a word from you before I left Mobile. I take it you got my letter?"

"Yes, we got it," she said. "I can't say we were pleased."

"Well, I knew it might cause a problem, but . . ."

"Sit," she said.

Hamilton sat in the straight-backed chair facing the door, glancing about the room again as he did so. Caroline followed his gaze with her own as he looked at the frayed, blue loveseat and the small, bare table before it.

"I stopped in the store and asked where you lived." He paused. "I've lived in some places about like this."

"We like it fine, thank you," Caroline said shortly. "It suits us. I'll get Aiken up now. He sleeps sometimes in the afternoon."

"Can I help?"

"No. I'll get one of the little negras around the store."

"I can do it, Sister. I remember how."

"If you must."

She followed him, ducking as she did so, into Aiken's tiny room. There, crouched beside him, she felt for an instant like a child again, hiding in one of the stable stalls, planning some new adventure with her brother. She remembered arguing once over whether they should go out and holler "snake" again in back of the house. But he'd said no, they had done that too many times already. And they had.

She called Aiken's name, waking him. His eyes flashed after

he'd turned his head toward them. His bent body remained still, outlined beneath the sheet.

"Hello, Aiken," Hamilton said.

Aiken looked up at Caroline. He lay silent at first, while he blinked and focused. Then he lifted his large head slightly from the pillow and stared at Hamilton.

"You came after all. Hoped you might show some good sense. But you never have showed much of that."

Hamilton drew a long breath, as if he were getting ready to argue or shout, but he only asked quickly if he could help Aiken from the bed.

"No," Aiken replied, "both of you just get the hell out. I ain't through with my sleep!"

When they had shuffled from the room in their crouching, hiding positions and stood finally erect, Hamilton stretched his arms out in front of him and pulled his shoulders back. The small bones of his elbows and wrists popped, and Caroline thought again how old they'd gotten. She followed her brother back into the front room.

"How long will you be staying?" she asked.

Hamilton studied her. "Until Sunday morning this visit," he said. Then he added slowly, "But I'll be back."

She quickly turned her face from him and looked out through the screen door, staring at the big oak between the house and the store. He repeated the words in a softer voice, sounding as if he were making a wish, but she realized that it was also a test.

"Where will you stay?"

"I'll find a room. There are some good people left."

"I'm sure you will find some place. Maybe you better go and look before it gets too late."

"All right, Sister." He looked out the door. "I guess I should. Did anyone know I was coming?"

"We told no one."

Hamilton pushed open the screen and picked up the suitcase from where it sat on Caroline's reading chair. "If I'm not back tonight, I'll see you both tomorrow."

Caroline said nothing.

She watched Hamilton walk toward the store, stepping over the dead tree limbs as he did so. She felt tired then, as if someone had made her do hard work all day. It suddenly occurred to her that she felt guilty, but she knew that she had no reason to. Hamilton had made his choices; she hadn't made them for him.

She stayed inside that night and set her plans to do so until Hamilton was gone. She didn't want people seeing them together or questioning her about him, saying they had seen him, wanting to know how he was. As long as he stayed in Riverfield she would feel trapped by his presence, as if she were the criminal.

She sat up with Aiken in the front room that night and waited to see if Hamilton would come. The temperature in the room rose. The night air seemed still, fixed, as if weighted by the heat. She sipped a small glass of the brandy, and she noticed each time the clock on the wall reached the hour or the half hour. Aiken watched her, but he didn't say anything. Occasionally she went over to his chair and wiped the sweat from his face with a damp rag. At ten o'clock she heard steps on the wooden ramp. Aiken stared at the door. Caroline wished that she knew what she would say, but it was only the boy who had been working on the mower; he entered the house in his usual shy manner.

"Is you ready for me to put you to bed, Mr. Aiken?" he asked.

"Yes, take me on, Isaac. I've had enough of this damn sitting." He peered at Caroline, implying, she knew, that it was her fault they had waited to no avail. The boy rolled the chair easily into Aiken's room, as if it traveled in its own worn ruts.

Caroline sat up alone for a few more minutes. She remembered getting angry once at Hamilton when they had been very small. She couldn't remember why. They had been behind the house, and she had picked up a stick and hit him. He'd begun to cry, and it had surprised her that he did. Then their mother came out, screaming, "What's wrong? What's going on out here?" Caroline had looked at Hamilton and then to her mother and said calmly, "Brother hit his head on this stick I've got in my hand." When they'd gotten older they had laughed about the incident.

Hamilton didn't come.

Finally she rose and walked to her room, feeling a strange mixture of anxiety and relief, each diluted by the warm, dark brandy that had filled her glass.

The morning began as the evening had ended. There was nothing she could do but wait in the tiny cell of the front room as the cool morning hours warmed into the afternoon.

At half-past-three, the afternoon heat reaching its zenith, she heard Hamilton's quiet step on the porch, then the screen door go back. She sat with a damp rag in her hand, wiping her face and arms. She was alone; Aiken was out riding in his chariot.

Hamilton looked to the rag and asked if she felt well.

"Well enough to deal with things," she said. "Go ahead and sit."

"I found a room in Aunt Janey's old house," he said as he sat and his glance again searched the room. "Sarah Ann and her husband put me up. They seemed glad to see me."

Caroline was silent.

Hamilton went on, as if his only comfort were in the sound of his own voice. "They told me that when I come back I can stay with them until I find a place."

"So you told them your plans?"

"Yes, Sister, I did."

"Did you tell anyone else?"

"I've just been seeing people," he said, not answering. "It does me good to be back here with people I know, people I've thought about every day for years. Today I feel I never really left."

"There are reasons why things have been as they have," she said as she moved the damp rag over her forehead. "And why things should continue as they are."

Hamilton looked at her angrily. "Why?"

The screen door opened suddenly and Aiken rolled awkwardly into the room, pushed by a different black youth. The boy looked younger, not as strong as Isaac, and had difficulty getting the wheels of the chair over the sill. Hamilton rose, grabbed the front of the chair, and pulled it toward him, looking directly into Aiken's face; then, after situating the chair, he stood erect and reached into his pocket.

"I pay him," Aiken said sharply. "Keep your damn money."

The boy left.

"It looks like it's time for our talk," Aiken said then.

"He wants to know why he can't move back," Caroline said quietly.

"Yes," Hamilton began. "I wish someone would tell me. Since Mother's dead I don't see why I can't."

"It was Mother's feeling that you should never bring further disgrace on us," Caroline said.

"I didn't steal any money, Caroline. It's ridiculous to carry this thing on."

She didn't answer immediately. After wiping her face with the cloth, she turned toward the door, carefully folded the piece of material, then unfolded it, delicately, as if it were fine lace. She began speaking slowly. "Whether you did or didn't . . ."

"You know I didn't," Hamilton said, cutting her off. "Mother worked in the post office that day. I never filled in for her in the morning, or the afternoon either. I only said I did. We all know why. I'm the one who got two years in Kilby."

"It doesn't make any difference if you took the money or not. What people think, what people perceive, that's . . ."

"That sounds like something you learned at Mother's knee. Look where that thinking got me. Got this whole damn family. Appearance. Remember when Mother started to wear corsets?"

"Hush, Hamilton, just hush," she said.

"Even while she was pregnant with Aiken?"

"Shut up," Aiken said. "That's enough."

Hamilton sat back in his chair looking thinner and paler. Caroline wiped the perspiration from her face and sipped from her glass. The dark brandy formed in beads above her lip. She spoke her words slowly.

"This family doesn't have what it used to."

"That's a fact."

"But there are people who still know us, and know where we came from, and as long as we conduct ourselves properly, people will continue to know."

"You mean remember." His voice trailed off as he turned his head from her and examined his open, empty hands.

Caroline took a deep breath, trying to fill herself with courage, but the void seemed suddenly larger than her thin body. She remembered once when their mother had been standing above her on the stairs leading up to the observatory, shouting down at her because she had wrecked the car. It hadn't been her fault. She'd been trying to make that clear for several days, but their mother continued to harass her about it. Hamilton had come running up from the floor below and had stood beside her, shouting, telling their mother to leave her alone, that it had not been something she could help. She'd loved him for what he'd done. Later she'd tried to thank him, had walked into his room to tell him just how much his help had meant to her, but her chest had suddenly felt empty, with nothing there to draw the breath it took to utter even the smallest thanks.

The words she began to speak now had an almost unendurable hollowness. "This house suits us. We get on fine." She paused, took another breath. "If you move back here, we can't stop you. But you're not welcome."

Hamilton looked over at Aiken, who seemed to have withdrawn into the only part of his body that functioned. "What do you say, Aiken?"

"I won't treat you any better than the nigger boys that push my chair," he answered, his words springing stronger than Caroline's, coming from a source she felt she no longer had.

Caroline met Hamilton's gaze as he turned toward her, again seeing in his features something of her own, something gone now.

"Why does it have to be this way?" he asked.

She didn't reply. She wiped her forehead again with the damp cloth. Hamilton stood quickly and pushed open the screen door, its rusted spring creaking. He looked at them only once more; then he walked out, easing the screen shut behind him.

Caroline sat across from Aiken. Motionless. The heat in the room and the brandy within her held the final question inside her head, making it ring against the fragile inner walls of her ears before it fell away into the void.

The Minister

H E STOOD IN THE PULPIT, sweating in his robe and
collar in the small Episcopal church and, silent for the moment, looked out again at his congregation, which was larger
this afternoon than the usual ten or eleven people who showed
up every other Sunday in Riverfield. He did not really like coming down here to this little community; he preferred his regular
church in Valhia, where he preached every Sunday in the cool
of air conditioning. Someone now quietly muffled a cough, and
there was the sound of shuffling feet. A young mother near
the front, whose name he could not recall, shifted her sleeping
baby from one arm to the other, and the older gray-haired
woman beside her seemed to look at him with puzzlement.
He knew that he paused too often, and that this probably
made them as uncomfortable and aware of his inexperience and
youth as he felt when they came in for counseling or when they

called him Father Meyers; the title was so hard to get used to.

The fact that there were more faces than normal had surprised him so much that at first he could not distinguish the new faces from the old. And even now he saw only what he always saw—solemn, blank looks that reminded him more of the poorly carved faces of angels in cemeteries, those that lacked all shape and detail, than faces that were actually made of flesh and human features. Then, as always at this point, the copper taste of fear and apprehension that was so strong in his mouth when he first stepped into the pulpit left him. One swallow and his throat loosened, and he felt again the same unexplainable sense of disappointment replace his fear.

He looked down and found his place in his notes. "Consider Amnon, the son of David," he said. "David was a good man, and he taught his children the difference between good and evil in the eyes of God, but Amnon ignored what he had been taught and forced himself upon his half-sister, and his brother Absalom killed him for his act."

He wiped a bead of perspiration from his cheek and looked up, again searching the faces, and then he saw, in the space where a woodstove had once sat, a man in a wheelchair whom he did not recognize and whose face was anything but blank. He noticed the eyes first; they seemed to him as dark as charred wood. The brows above them grew thick and white, and the forehead, he saw, protruded farther than was normal, like a crag. His hair was thin, combed wet across a head that was large and square. He imagined later that the head had been crudely carved out of some oak tree stump—the skin on the powerful neck rough like bark, the face shaped from the heartwood. He could not understand how he had missed this face when he'd looked up earlier; it stared back at him so, as if to challenge, to say, I don't believe, the other faces near it serving only as a dull and undefined background, those expressionless stone angels. Here was the face that he had been looking for, and he felt a curiosity and an excitement rising in his blood.

After communion for the handful of members who regularly attended and took part in the ritual, he said a final prayer and stepped back into his vestry to wipe the perspiration from his face and gather himself. He then went outside to thank people for coming and looked for the old man, but did not see him anywhere. He wondered then where he had come from, who he was.

Sarah Ann Rutledge, a widow, was the church's caretaker; her son John rang the bell each Sunday and served as altar boy. She had not been at church that day, so the next afternoon he drove down to see if she had been ill. She answered the door wearing a brightly colored summer dress and long dangling earrings most women her age could not get away with wearing. They sat in her kitchen, and she explained that she'd been out of town the day before. He then asked about the old man.

She took a sip of wine first and lit her usual Camel cigarette. "His name's Aiken Reed, and he's from one of the old families around here," she said. "His mother was a Teclaw. They're old church members. He's been in the nursing home in Valhia for a long time—about ten years. I don't know what's keeping him alive, unless its just plain meanness." She laughed.

"Was he in an accident?" he said.

"No. Not that." She looked straight down into her glass of wine. "I don't know if I should say anything else. Besides, it's all just really nonsense—a lot of it anyway. What folks around here would call 'nigger superstition,' if you'll please pardon my use of that word."

"I want to hear. Tell me."

"He was born that way, if you want to know, paralyzed from the neck down. Except he can move his fingers on one hand a little. His mama was called Miss Amelia. I used to spend a lot of time up there at their big old house as a child and knew her pretty well. When she was carrying him, she didn't want to look big. She was getting older, heavier, and she was vain. So she'd get some of those black girls who worked for her to strap her up in a corset. They'd get behind her I've heard, and pull those strings as tight as they could, her hollering at them all the time to pull even tighter. And they did pull tighter because they were scared of her. She had a nasty tone that I've never heard the like of. All their black help used to swear that she was the devil." She stopped and stared into her wine, then looked up again. "I know it's hard to believe. They didn't mean it as any figure of speech either. They believed it.

"When she finally gave birth, she had twins, but one of them, a boy, was stillborn. Severely deformed. From what some of the girls said, it hardly looked human. The help swore, and I know this part is just pure foolishness, that it had little knobs on its head that looked like horns. She had it buried out in the back of the house that afternoon. No coffin, no funeral. She made Uncle Silas bury it. He was the only black help who stayed with her, and she told him to not let anyone know where the grave was—not her husband, or any of the children, and not even her. She didn't name it or talk about it. Uncle Silas never would, either. Aiken himself didn't even know about it until he was fully grown.

"So they said then, the blacks, that Aiken was a child of the devil. Said a child of the devil always dies in fire. And the old ones are sure that that's the way he'll go. I don't know if he was any child of the devil or not, but he did grow up to be mean. He bit his sister Caroline one time. Bit her when she bent over near his chair. And he's got big square teeth, too, like a horse or a mule. This was after they were older and had to live in that shack out behind Anderson's store—after they'd had to sell the family home. He tried to kill her once, too. Got one of the little black boys who pushed him around in his chair to hand him his sister's .32 from out of a drawer, and he tried to pull the trigger with those fingers of his that he can move a little. The pistol wouldn't fire, though.

"After Caroline died, he went into the nursing home. There was no one else to care for him. He'd had a brother, but the brother was dead by that time."

She stared into her half-empty glass a moment, then looked up at him and studied his face. He wondered what she saw in his expression. His hands were tingling, and the blood that had risen in his face began now to slowly drain away. He felt both a sense of horror and curiosity, and each made him uncomfortable.

He stood outside the Riverfield church, waiting, trying to avoid the wasps that hovered in a mean swarm near the front entrance. There was only the usual handful of people this time, nothing like the crowd two weeks before. Disappointed, he finally went inside to his tiny vestry that always smelled as if pesticides had once been stored there.

At exactly three o'clock he stepped out and took his seat while Sarah Ann's son John lit the candles. When he stood up to begin, he scanned the congregation and saw that there were a few more faces, people who must have come in at the last minute. He looked toward the first pew to his right, and there, between the pew and the wall, he saw the rough-carved face he had been hoping for. Sarah Ann was sitting next to him.

He preached with more vigor than usual, and at the end, after giving communion at the rail, he decided to go down to Aiken. The old man kept his head lowered, his eyes averted. He wondered if he had made a mistake by approaching him. Finally Aiken looked up, his black eyes intense, perhaps a trace of anger in them. He fed him the wafer and brought the chalice up to the dry lips, tilting it. The lips did not seem to part, and as he held the cup he imagined that Aiken was not letting the wine flow into his mouth but was merely holding it against his lips, letting it drain back into the cup. He removed the chalice, wiped it, and saw wine stains down the front of the wrinkled shirt. Aiken would not look at him now. He turned and as he walked away he wondered if Aiken might even be holding the wafer in his mouth still, waiting to spit it out once he left the church. For an instant he remembered doing the same thing when he was a child. It had only been a kind of game he had played, but his father had whipped him, he recalled.

He arrived at the nursing home late the next day, carrying some magazines that he'd bought at the drugstore. After asking for the room number, he walked down the hall to 110. He recognized the ammonia smell of disinfectant, but there was another odor that he could not name, something strong but not quite definable. The smell made him think of sickness and age. And death.

He knocked on the door and entered at the sound of the grunt that came from the other side. Aiken was sitting in his chair with his back toward the door, looking out the storm window at the parking lot.

"I've come to see you," he said. "It was good to have you in church again the other day."

A grunt first. Then, "So the preacher has come," he said, craning his neck around.

"May I sit down?"

No answer.

"I brought you some magazines. I thought you could get someone to turn the pages," he said as he lay them on the nightstand.

There was no response. He took a seat across from Aiken and looked into the hard face. He imagined for a moment the dead twin.

"Can I get you anything while I'm here? Do anything for you?"

"They got nurses here," Aiken said.

"Is this a bad time? Would you rather I hadn't come?"

No answer again. He heard only Aiken's deep breath.

"I could turn the magazine pages for you, if you'd like."

Aiken still did not speak.

"Maybe you'd like to hear about some of the news around town?"

"The nurses tell me things."

"All right then."

He sat for a while longer. A nurse came in finally and gave Aiken some water and adjusted him in his chair, pulling the sheepskin up behind his back. She commented on his company, but that brought no response either.

Not long after the nurse left, he got up. "If there's nothing I can do for you, I suppose I'll go," he said in a tone as level as he could possibly make it. He did not wait for any kind of comment, but walked out the door.

He had wanted only to provide Aiken with company, he thought, to bring some kind of variety to the routine of his days. He felt angry for the silence he'd been shown, and he didn't understand why Aiken had been so belligerent. But if Aiken would reject communion, the body and the blood, wouldn't he also reject a minister?

As he pulled away from the parking lot, out onto the quiet street, he recalled for a moment how he had been famous for his own silences at the seminary, and that people had been bothered by this, made uncomfortable.

Toward the end of the week he dreamed about Aiken, which he found odd because he usually did not dream, or at least he did not remember his dreams. He recalled having been in a room, not a hospital or nursing home room, but one that was bare and that somehow put him in mind of an old mental institution, something from out of the last century. The ceiling was high and there were long, narrow windows at the top of one wall. All the walls were plaster, and they were painted a deep red that made him think of rust, or even dried blood. He sat in a wooden chair and Aiken sat across from him, interrogation style. *Why did you try to shoot her?* he kept saying. *She was your sister. Did you want to kill her?* Aiken did not respond; he looked only at the floor, seemingly bored. Out of frustration his voice became louder. *Could you kill someone?* he said. *Well? Would you kill me?* Aiken was still silent. *You want me to leave you alone? I won't,* he said, becoming angrier.

When he awakened he pulled the covers off himself and sat up in bed. He kept hearing the voice in his dream, the way it grew louder, and he recognized it as being familiar, but he knew that it was not *his* voice. The questions were his, and he had to admit, the anger, too, but the voice . . .

And then he placed it. When he was young and in trouble for some adolescent behavior, such as not eating his communion wafer, his father, a small man who'd looked always as if he were working on some minute and difficult task, and who, the last year of his life, had been confined to a wheelchair of his own because of arthritis, would ask him over and over, "Why did you do it? How could you?" And his father's voice would grow louder with each question, each accusation, as his had in the dream. At times like these he would become so angry that he would grip hard the arms of whatever chair he had been made to sit in, and he would feel that if he exerted just the slightest amount of extra pressure he could break the arms in half. He'd felt at the time that he would have done anything to make his father stop. But he thought now that these were simply boyhood aggressions, nothing more. They were best forgotten; certainly they were nothing to be thinking about in the middle of the night.

Several days later he again pushed open the heavy door to Aiken's room and sat down directly across from him, just as he had in his dream, and in fact he thought for a moment about the dream; it was not something he could forget. The thing he remembered most, strangely enough, was not Aiken's bored expression, but the sharp anger in his own voice that reminded him of the edge he heard in Aiken's speech.

"You came back," Aiken said. "You like this godforsaken place?" He laughed.

"God doesn't forsake, Aiken. And yes, I'm back, but not just to visit. I'd like to take you out for the day. If you'll go."

"Where?" Aiken looked at him suspiciously, twisting his thick neck.

"To Tuscaloosa. We could drive up and get something to eat," he said, hoping he didn't sound too anxious. He was not used to telling lies, even partial ones. The fact was he had planned more than simply eating lunch.

"Anything would be better than the food here. Hogs eat better."

"So you'll go?" he said, a little surprised.

"All right."

The night before, he'd taken out one of the seats in the church van so that there would be room if the answer was yes. A black orderly pushed the chair now up the one-by-six boards he'd bought and into the van.

"You have a nice ride," the orderly said.

Aiken grunted.

There was little talk on the way up. Aiken sat behind him and this made conversation difficult, but they were almost there now, and he had to tell Aiken what he had in mind.

"Would you like to get around on your own some, Aiken?" he said, wondering if this were the right way to begin. He watched Aiken's face in the mirror and saw the sudden scowl, like what one might expect to see only on the face of a convict.

"What are you talking about?"

"You can move the fingers on your right hand, I've noticed. Maybe enough to operate an electric wheelchair. I'd like to see if you can handle one. I know where there's a medical supply house. I've talked to someone there already. It's up to you."

He saw Aiken's expression soften for a moment, and just before the hardness crept back into it, he thought he saw the eyes flash for one instant, like a prisoner contemplating an escape. He knew better than to speak. The wrong word might ruin any chance. He stopped for the first redlight, then turned in the direction of the supply house.

"Can't afford it," Aiken finally said.

"They have a used one. And donations have been made. Will you try it?"

"I might. Maybe I can find a place to hide from all those damn nurses who plague me."

At the supply house a bearded, heavy-set man helped him lift Aiken into the chair. He took Aiken's hand, surprised at how soft it felt, and placed it on the control knob. Aiken pushed it and the chair rolled forward. He saw again the quick flash in Aiken's eyes just before Aiken closed them into a squint, as if a strong white light that was his own pleasure made them shut.

He rolled himself toward the door, turned, then came back. "Why are you doing this?" His look was accusing.

"Only to help you," he said.

"I believe that's the second lie you've told today, Preacher. You best watch out or you'll be going to hell with me."

He loaded the old chair into the back of the van, then helped Aiken guide himself up the boards and into his place behind the driver's seat. He wondered if Aiken was right about his telling a lie. He didn't like to think so.

Later they sat inside a screened-in porch and ate catfish at a restaurant by the river. He fed Aiken bites of fish between his own, aware in a way he hadn't been of just how helpless Aiken was, and he remembered for a moment feeding his father near the end, remembered how his father twisted his head back and forth and seemed to resent each bite that was fed him. But he had made him eat, no matter how unpleasant the task had gotten.

"I saw Sarah Ann the other day," he said. "She told me to ask you about the church, how it came to Riverfield. Would you?"

Aiken twisted his neck and eyed him slowly, as if he were making a decision. "You might not like what you hear, but I'll tell you." He laughed softly. "The church was brought from over across the Tennahpush River. This was a long time ago that I'm talking about, before the War. They took it apart in sections to move it. Put it on a barge."

He studied Aiken as he spoke. Perhaps his earlier silences had been a kind of test; perhaps he was lonely and finally wanted some relief, even from a minister.

"It was my great-grandfather, Jason Teclaw, what had it done. He was my mother's grandfather. They had kicked him out the Methodist Church. First said he mistreated his niggers, that he beat them too hard and too much, that he didn't feed them enough. I'm talking about slaves here," he said, leveling his eyes. "Then he went and opened up a saloon in the cellar beneath his house. That was the last straw, I guess. That's what Mama said. I don't know really about his beating the niggers too much. Course when I was little the old post still stood, where they were beaten I mean." He stopped and looked at Meyers again. His eyes were charcoal dark beneath his heavy brows and protruding forehead. "Mama *said* it was the whipping post, anyway. I figured she knew. She used to threaten to whip us at it." He laughed again, rougher this time.

"When they kicked him out, he said, 'To hell with all you. I'll buy my own damn church.' And he did. Bought it. Moved it. Set it up again. And then brought him in his own preacher. The house he lived in and had the saloon under is Sarah Ann's. You ever been in there?"

Meyers pictured himself sitting in the kitchen with Sarah Ann, at the table, and he then thought about the church itself. Even though he hadn't liked it at first, he had come to think of the church as his almost, though he knew that it, like all churches, really belonged to God. Now, hearing its history, hearing about the connection between it and Aiken's family, the church seemed somehow less his—less God's even. It seemed marked by its past. He imagined now that the church would look somehow different to him the next time he saw it.

They made the drive back, and he felt pleased with himself for having drawn Aiken out. The trip had been a success, he felt. Next time he would ask the questions that had been on his mind. He would learn something about the Aiken behind the misshapen face.

After a day of visiting sick, elderly church members in their homes, and counseling a young couple, he drove down to River-field and told Sarah Ann about his trip with Aiken, then asked to see the old saloon. She took him outside, and he followed. She swung open the two doors built below a window and, peering in, he saw only a dirt floor. The smell struck him hard. It was as if the air had been contaminated with some kind of gas or poison long ago and strong traces of it remained. The smell, he noticed, was somehow familiar to him. It was just the smell of something old, he told himself. He then imagined men with beards and drooping mustaches sitting at a long bar and tables, smoking cigars and drinking bourbon, telling rough jokes and stories. He even imagined a prostitute walking across the room. But it was the smell that came strongest. He realized that it was the same sort of smell as in his vestry, that pesticide odor. It wasn't confined to only one place.

He had been to the church earlier, alone. It had looked the same to him, but he'd *felt* something different about it as he'd walked between the pews and then up to the altar. He knew that except for the space heaters and the woodstove that had been removed, the church looked now just as it had when Jason Teclaw moved it, and that the light coming through the stained glass windows was no different in quality than it had been over a hundred years ago, when men owned other men and were given allowance to beat them. Standing there, looking at this light, he'd thought he felt the presence of Teclaw, and he had not minded this. In fact, it pleased him somehow, and he'd found this troublesome, upsetting.

He realized now that there was something else strange about the smell in the cellar. It wasn't just that he recognized it as being similar to the smell in his vestry; he felt as if the power of the smell awakened something deep within his memory, from his childhood maybe, but he did not know what. Or perhaps it wasn't a memory at all that was being called up, but something else from deep inside him, from a place as deep as this cellar, perhaps the place where that copper taste came from. He opened the door wider and imagined again men drinking, even shouting. And then he thought again about the beatings Aiken had mentioned. He began to imagine them, and he would not allow himself to simply picture the scene from a distance, like something from an old movie where the camera angle might avoid a man's back; he forced himself to look at the hard images: the hand of Teclaw, the strips of leather, the bloody pulp of a man's black skin. And suddenly he saw Aiken there too, *standing* beside the post, watching. He saw the charcoal darkness in Aiken's eyes, what he had come to think of as hate; or maybe it was more than that. He took a breath and became aware again of the gas-like smell.

"What's that odor?" he asked.

"It's just musty down here, like you'd expect."

Aiken was sitting in the new chair when he walked into the nursing home room. He had not come for a simple visit this time either. He had another request to make, one that he felt Aiken would be surprised to hear—just as he'd surprised himself with the idea.

"How are you today?" he asked. "I brought you some more magazines."

"Put them on the nightstand," Aiken said, and then was silent.

"Well, may I sit down?"

"Why not? I am," he said.

"There's a tent revival outside of town this week. Have you heard?"

"I've heard."

"Have you ever been to one?"

"When I was a child. They were something of a social event."

"I know they're common around here, or used to be. I've never been to one. You could say I'm curious. I'd like to go one night. I've been assured there will be preaching only, no fake healing. Would you go?" he said, hoping again that he did not sound too anxious.

"You trying to get me saved, Preacher?" Aiken looked at him through squinted eyes. "You figure a little fiery preaching might get through to me if your good works don't?" He laughed.

The suddenness of the question surprised him, and he felt as if Aiken's narrowed eyes somehow allowed the man to see into him as clearly as one sees through a piece of newly washed glass. For a moment he did not know what to say. "Well, it never hurts to hear God's word," he said, "and I thought you might want to get out."

"So it's mostly just my social life you're concerned with?" He laughed again.

The following evening they sat under a large tent on the end of a row and near the front. People from Valhia walked past. They wore mostly jeans and work clothes. A few people spoke, surprised to see him, but seemingly pleased. Many he did not recognize, but watched them mill around and talk in small groups. There were perhaps two hundred people, mostly white.

It began with singing. They all stood and shared the hymnals that had been passed out. Meyers declined one and mumbled along to "Onward Christian Soldiers" as best he could. He looked to see if Aiken might be singing, or trying to, but he was not.

There was an opening prayer led by a young man in shirt-sleeves, more singing, then a collection. He made an offering when the plate filled with fives and tens was handed past, wondering exactly where his money would go.

Then an older man in a coat and tie with thick graying hair worn a little too long walked out. Brother Johnson, he called himself. He stood at the pulpit and began to preach, and just like the preachers on television, his voice began to rise in pitch and volume.

"There is wickedness in this world, Brothers and Sisters. Do you believe it?"

"Yes. Amen," people mumbled.

"Look at the children of Israel. They were God's chosen. But what did they do? There was evil in them, and they did evil in the sight of the Lord."

"Amen."

He picked up his Bible now and shook it above the pulpit. "Look in the Book of Judges. They forsook the Lord and served Baal and Astaroth. And the anger of the Lord was hot against Israel. So he judged them and delivered them into the hands of spoilers."

He paused for a moment, then drew himself up and shouted, "Are you ready to be judged? Do you want to be ready?"

"Yes. Amen."

Meyers listened, and, despite himself, his blood quickened. He looked at Aiken, but there was nothing in the face that he could read. He found himself studying Aiken's profile, the line of the thick neck and jaws, the shape of the head. Through the thin white hair he saw that the skull was not shaped smoothly. There were flat places and sudden rises. He thought of the dead twin—what the blacks had said about its misshapened head, and the preacher's words about the children of Israel rang in his ears.

The preacher went on to describe the hell that would be awaiting them if they were judged and found lacking. There were more hymns, and then the call. "Come down and give yourself to Jesus," the preacher said. "He is waiting on you. Won't you come?"

Only a few went. He did not expect Aiken to go, and he realized that he didn't want him to. His time with Aiken was long from over, and if Aiken ever gave himself, *he* wanted to be the instrument. He hoped God would forgive him for this sin of pride.

They sat while the crowd slowly made its way out. Aiken seemed not to have moved the whole time.

"Was it anything like you remember?" he said.

"They ain't changed much."

"Sarah Ann has invited us to eat with her after church this Sunday. She said that we could all eat in the backyard since the steps up to the house are all so high. Said it would be like a picnic. She really would love to have you come."

"All right."

He was pleased that Aiken would agree so readily. He didn't know if now was the time or not, but there were the questions he wanted to ask.

"We've got a bit of a wait it looks like. I'd like to know something about your family," he said. He paused and then added, "Your mother must have been a strong woman."

Aiken gave him a careful look and did not speak. His eyes were narrowed again and he held his head at an odd angle. "She was strong."

He wanted to proceed carefully. "Sarah Ann told me that you lived with your sister a long time. After you lost the old house."

"Yes. I did. Did she tell you that Caroline and I didn't get along?"

"Yes. But she never really said why. And I didn't ask."

"So you're asking now."

"No."

"Yes, you are. That's why you brought her up."

Meyers was silent.

"Sarah Ann probably told you I bit Caroline once. She likes to tell that one." He grunted. "I bit her so damn hard. I wouldn't let go. They were afraid I might have given her blood poisoning." He craned his head forward. "I wish I had," he said.

Meyers winced.

"I tried to shoot her once. Sarah Ann tell you about it?"

"No," he said, and realized that his face hadn't registered the surprise it should.

"*Another* lie." He laughed. "Maybe you're not so different from me after all, even if you don't know it."

He did not answer this.

"So let me tell you. I got one of the little nigger boys that pushed me around in my old chair to hand me her little pistol, a lady's revolver. I can move these fingers pretty well sometimes. When she came into the room, she didn't even see it in my hand. She was probably drunk." He looked at Meyers. "Didn't fire. The damn thing. I tried again, but then she saw the gun and screamed. She grabbed it from me, and I thought she might use it on me. 'You don't have the guts,' I said."

He found that he was looking at Aiken's head again while he spoke, studying the slightly misshapened skull.

"I suppose you'd like to know if I had a reason to shoot her," Aiken said. "Well, I had reason."

"What was it?"

"You don't have to know everything."

"Did you really want to kill her, or only to wound her? I need to know at least that much."

"Does all this sound as Old Testament to you as the preaching we just heard?" He looked, Meyers thought, as if he were studying him, trying to answer his own set of questions about this strange minister who brought him to tent revivals.

"You haven't answered my question."

Aiken laughed. "And I won't."

He stood. "God has a place for you, Aiken. There is such a thing as salvation. And it doesn't have to be gotten in a tent."

"Does he have a place for you?" Aiken asked.

The question seemed an odd one, and he did not try to respond.

"I just have one more thing I'd like to ask. At that communion, did you . . . drink the wine? Did you swallow it?"

"You know nothing," Aiken said, and he then began laughing.

Meyers dreamed again that night, and he was somehow aware of the dream as he dreamed it. He first heard himself shouting, and this time he recognized the voice as his own. Aiken sat across from him in the wheelchair as he had before with his large head tilted backward, laughing at him in fits that grew steadily louder, saying *You know nothing* between each laugh. He gripped tight the arms of his own chair, just as when his father used to scold him. *Stop it, damnit,* he said. But the laughter continued, and his own shouting became stronger. Soon he found himself standing over Aiken, and then, still aware that he was dreaming but unable to stop, he began striking Aiken repeatedly against the side of the head with a metal object that he soon realized was a small revolver. When he finally stopped, he stared down at the tilted head, saw the swollen face, and recognized a body that he was afraid was no longer paralyzed but lifeless.

He woke then, got out of bed, and walked unsteadily to his kitchen where he sat down at the table without turning on a light. He would not let himself think about what he had dreamed. He looked out the window through his dim reflection and into the dark and tried to calm the fear he felt inside.

His sermon that Sunday was on the nature of evil. And for once the tension and nervousness he always felt just before preaching had *not* disappeared into boredom as he stepped into the pulpit and began. The taste of copper hadn't left him. He felt a kind of elation that ran through his body like heat from a low fever. "Evil does exist among us," he said. "We ate of the tree of knowledge. We do not live in Eden, but east of Eden. And Cain did slay his brother Abel." He was not shouting or gesturing wildly, but he was aware that his words echoed those he'd heard several nights before, and he began to wonder what was happening to him.

All through the sermon he felt Aiken's dark gaze, but he had decided that he would not let it deter him, not again. When the time came he walked straight to where Aiken sat. Aiken stared at him, then grimaced. He lifted the cup and Aiken took the lip of the chalice in his teeth, clinched them hard, and he watched as the red wine drained along the corners of Aiken's mouth and down his shirt. This time he was almost certain.

After the service he and Aiken sat at the picnic table behind Sarah Ann's house. The smell of the sliced roast, green-bean casserole, potato salad, and dinner rolls drew flies, but they managed, he and Sarah Ann, to keep most of them fanned away. Wasps darted dangerously close.

He felt Aiken's gaze now from the end of the table. His breath grew short, but he managed a blessing.

Sarah Ann got up and served Aiken's plate.

"You've fixed this nice meal," he said, "brought it out here and now you should sit and enjoy it. I'll take care of Aiken—if he doesn't mind," he added with a determined note in his voice.

"That would be nice," she said. "If you want to do it."

Aiken looked past the both of them. "I don't care who feeds me."

He served his own plate and then moved down the bench closer to Aiken and began to cut the food on Aiken's plate into small bites. After finishing he took the fork and pushed a piece of roast into the open, waiting mouth. While Aiken chewed, he managed to make himself eat.

Sarah Ann began to talk, first about getting some repair work done on the church roof, then about things going on in Riverfield. He hardly listened to her, which was unusual. He found himself concentrating on Aiken's face as Aiken listened to Sarah Ann's stories. He kept feeding Aiken, first with bites of roast, then potato salad. Occasionally he took a few small bites from his own food. He fed Aiken another piece of roast; then, after breaking apart a dinner roll, he put a piece of bread into the open mouth with his fingers. He waited a moment, then lifted a glass to Aiken's lips, tilted it, and watched him take the water and swallow. He was no longer aware of Sarah Ann's voice; it was just another sound, like the passing of a car, or the sharp chattering of the birds and squirrels. Without realizing it, he took the remaining piece of Aiken's bread and put it into his own mouth. He lifted the heavy glass to take a drink and then thought of how he lifted the chalice during the communion ceremony. As he held the glass in front of him, he realized that he had eaten Aiken's bread. He felt suddenly as if the eating of this food were also a kind of odd communion. He stared at the man across from him and tasted on his tongue the remnants of Aiken's bread. He then pushed Aiken's plate away and quickly drank a swallow of water.

A car passed. He could hear it through the trees. Wasps swarmed under the eaves of the house and beneath the back steps. He watched them and then the cellar doors caught his attention. They were still open.

"Would you like me to finish helping Aiken?" he heard Sarah Ann ask.

"Yes. Please." He looked down at the uneaten food on his plate.

After the meal he helped Sarah Ann take the food and empty dishes inside. He was glad to be away from Aiken even for a short time.

Later, two of Sarah Ann's friends came by, older women who were church members, but he hardly paid any attention to the conversation. He only nodded his head occasionally. By the time the company left it was nearly dark. He loaded Aiken into the van using the two one-by-six boards for a ramp, then thanked Sarah Ann again for her hospitality. He pulled out of the drive, and in the very last of the twilight he noticed a large bank of clouds in the distance.

By the time he was halfway to Valhia, it was dark, so dark that against the blacktop of the old bridge he did not see the calf until a peel of thunder brought with it a flash of heat lightning. He jerked the wheel too quickly and heard then not another peel of thunder, but the splintering of the wooden guardrail.

He was not sure which he became aware of first—the yellow then purple hues of light that came and went over the cloud bank, and that later made him think of the sky as bruised, or of the sharp pain in the small of his back that pulsed up his spine in currents and ran out into his shoulders as if along thin filaments. He reached slowly out and, trying to move himself, grabbed at the limestone creek bank. It broke in his hands like pieces of chalk. He tried to move his legs and they would not respond. Afraid that he might be paralyzed, he looked down, squinting to see in the dark, and forced the muscles in his legs and ankles to work. The pain grew more intense, but he watched himself move each of his feet, first the right and then, with not quite as much pain, the left. He uttered a short prayer of thanks. Then, because he had thought *paralyzed,* he suddenly remembered Aiken, who he knew must still be in the van.

In the flash of the heat lightning that came again, he saw clearly the wrecked church van against the creek bank, the splintered wooden guardrail, and the calf still standing on the bridge. He realized he had been thrown by the impact. Then he smelled gas. He called Aiken's name and, getting no answer, whispered another short prayer.

He pushed against the limestone and slid on down into the water. It came only up to his knees. The jar of hitting the creek bed sent spasms of pain up his back, and he knew that he could move more quickly if he crawled toward the van than if he tried to walk, so he lowered himself into the shallow water, keeping his head just above its surface. He noticed a stronger smell of gas, then the pulse of night sounds. There were bullfrogs croaking farther up the creek, and he heard a hound barking in the distance. Above the dog's baying, he thought he heard a cry.

"Aiken," he called.

Another muffled cry came, like someone calling from out of a deep dream.

He crept against the current, and there in the black water he saw reflected another flash of heat lightning. There was no thunder now, no sound of any kind, only silent light. He watched a small, steady reflection of orange begin to grow in the water, and he realized that this was *not* heat lightning.

In that moment before the flames took the van he heard Aiken's strong bleating cries; then the flames began to pour from the broken windows. Helpless, he pushed away from the burning wreck just as an explosion sent fire above the bridge. He could not help but think of the van as a kind of funeral pyre. He lifted his hands out of the water and pressed his palms against his warm face. The creek's gentle current helped carry him past the bridge. Finally he dragged his feet along the creek's bottom, stopping himself, his back shot with pain, then managed to crawl up onto the bank; it was not steep here as on the other side. He could still see the burning van, but could no longer hear Aiken's cries.

"A child of the devil will die—*has died*—in fire," he thought. For a moment he imagined Aiken as an infant, naked and crippled, lying beside the dead twin with its arms and legs bent at unnatural angles, its head marked by the two knobs, its mouth open. He thought of Aiken's body in the van, what it must look like, and it seemed to him now that these bodies that he imagined had finally become one body. Aiken was now that mangled thing that had been buried in an unmarked grave.

Lying there on the bank, wet and muddy, he watched the flames of the van die, saw their orange reflection grow smaller and smaller on the rippling black water. He remembered Aiken's rough voice and his silences, and he recalled how he had eaten the bread, remembered the taste of it, and he remembered, too, the dream he'd had and what he had done in it. He latched onto an image then that he'd had before and that ran like a movie reel in his mind, only now the image was changed. He saw Aiken standing watching those lashes strike, one after another, across a man's bare back, but now there were other figures crowded together. He saw church members, including Sarah Ann, their faces sharp and distinct, all entranced, standing in a half-circle and watching the spectacle with almost a kind of enjoyment, their stares hard enough to break stone. And he saw himself, a figure in dark garments who stood apart from the crowd, but who watched just as intently—as intently as Aiken even. He became afraid suddenly, frightened at the fact that he could imagine all he was seeing, and, worse, that he could see himself there. He tasted copper on his tongue; then he saw his dark figure walk toward the congregation members and he became lost among them.

Violent light flashed. It looked, he thought, like some kind of gas-fire. The light illuminated the van, the large white oak on the bank above, the barbed-wire fence that ran along the creek on one side; and it made everything look different somehow, as if everything in his sight were now part of a new countryside. He could see it all very clearly. When he considered the vision he'd had, he did not have to question why he'd seen himself in it. And now the dream made sense to him. "Maybe you're not so different from me after all," Aiken had said.

He began to crawl toward the road, through the grass and weeds and broken bottles. He hoped that someone he knew, perhaps from his church, would come along and see him. He breathed in the humid night air, pushed himself farther along the ground, and felt the rain begin to fall.

A Father and Son

HE ALMOST HADN'T COME. He'd wanted Alfonso to
ride along, but after stopping at just about every shack
down in Jackson Quarter, he hadn't been able to find him. It
didn't really matter; he'd been here alone before. He would be
all right.

From where Harlan Neely sat, he could feel each time the ball
bounced against one of the hollow places under the varnished
floor. Instead of a sharp, cracking ricochet, there was only a dead
thud, like someone tapping against a wall, looking for studs but
hitting the spots in between. He noticed that even though the
ball didn't bounce quite the same way, the bad spots didn't slow
the players down. They moved the ball quick, smooth. Breaking fast, they filled the lanes, always moving toward the basket.
Sometimes the mass of bodies was so thick and moved so quickly
under the goal that he could hardly follow them. He tried to

concentrate only on their uniforms and numbers as he kept the faded red separate from the orange. Then a player would take a shot and black arms would reach up, slapping for the ball, and hands would sometimes dart above the rim. Then a rebound, and the mass would hurl itself toward the other end of the court.

There were bleachers on both sides of the gym, reaching halfway up the walls, packed with people standing, yelling, their deep-voiced yells sometimes becoming chants. He searched the stands for the second time since he'd come in, but he didn't need to. He knew that his was the only white face. But they had seen him before, most of them anyway. They knew him. When he got home his father would want to know if he'd been the only white there. Maybe he'd lie this time and spare himself another angry speech.

When he was by himself he would usually sit, as he did now, at the end of the bleachers near the door. He'd wait until after the game started, then slip in and squeeze into a place down low. He would sit with his large, scuffed, untied shoes propped on the edge of the row in front of him, the cuffs of his khaki pants pulling up past his bare ankles. Tonight, while driving over, he had spilled a bottle of beer across his knees, and his pants were still wet and the smell strong. The people at the door had acted as if they hadn't wanted him to come in. One dark-skinned man in a green tie had eyed him carefully, like a policeman watching someone walking away down a dark street. Harlan ran a hand over his knees to see just how damp the spots still were, then felt his shirt pocket to be sure he had cigarettes.

Time-out was called. He stretched his arms in front of him, then clasped his hands behind his head and ran his fingers along the bottom of his cap, checking to be sure he could feel hair where the cap sat down on his head. He reached down and knocked dried mud off the side of one shoe.

They began moving down court again, driving hard for the basket. They moved quick, easy. He knew he'd never had that kind of grace. But he'd been a center; it hadn't been so important. He could see it was going to be close. Three minutes left. Only a four-point spread.

He remembered the last close game he had played in. Coach Morris had worked out an elaborate play for the final eleven seconds. He'd been squatting down, watching while Coach drew on the little board. "You mean if we score right now, we'll win?" he'd asked. "Well, yes, Harlan, that's right," Coach had said. He'd gotten the ball at almost half-court, then looked up at the goal. He knew he wasn't supposed to shoot, but the goal didn't seem too far. He glanced at Morris. The man just threw up his hands and shook his head. Six seconds left. He put his whole body into it, watched the ball sail. It felt right.

Afterward, they'd given him the game ball. Then, weeks later, several of them went down to Mardi Gras in Mobile. After returning, there had been the offer from the private college in Birmingham. His father had even seemed glad, didn't call him son of a bitch for a week. He went on a tour of the place. It was nice. Big open grounds with grass greener than a pasture, tall pines, red brick buildings that looked like they were scrubbed clean every day. But he didn't like to think about all of that anymore. There was no use in thinking about it. And too, when he thought that far back, it always brought memories of Barry.

There were only twenty seconds left now. The score had

stretched to a difference of eight, but it didn't really matter to Harlan who won. In the last minute or so the playing was sloppy. He heard the final buzzer after he had already walked out the door. The legs of his pants felt almost dry. Outside, the man in the green tie eyed him again as he walked past.

He spotted the two bottles of beer lying on the floor of his truck as he got in. He'd put them there to keep them hidden from people's view, and luckily they hadn't rolled and fallen through the rusted-out hole on the passenger's side. By the time he was on the second one, he'd driven six of the ten miles of narrow county road to Riverfield. Just at the top of the last big hill, his headlights caught two black cows, mixed, but mostly Angus, standing beside the blacktop. During the previous week he'd had to patch his own fence. A cow had gotten out, had broken several strands of the rusted wire. But he hadn't minded doing the work. He loved fooling with the cows, even though he only had thirty-five head and couldn't make any real money from them. He'd begun raising them a few years earlier when his father had told him that he could do whatever he wanted with the seventy acres they owned. Now the old man had begun to make a habit of saying that when he gave Harlan the land he sure as hell hadn't meant for him to quit everything else; said he had a more-than-grown-up son, a son who even was losing his hair, who hardly did a damn thing anymore. And why in the hell had Harlan gone and quit his job last year?

The dirt drive was coming up fast. He slowed the pickup, pumped the brake to the floor, and pulled the wheel hard to make the turn. The drive wound beside the pasture and ended in a grove of pines, where the small house he and his father shared stood directly beneath the trees.

He stopped his truck. The yellow porch light made the surrounding pines seem somehow darker. He put the truck in reverse, and set the emergency brake, remembering how having to release the brake irritated his father when the old man borrowed the truck. He got out and walked to the house. All the lights were off inside. From the porch, he felt his way to his room.

Breakfast was already made when Harlan woke up. Harlan could smell it. He walked into the kitchen, wearing the same khakis and shirt he'd worn the night before, his cap pulled low over his eyes. The spilled beer on his pants smelled stale.

His father stood in front of the stove laying the bacon out on a towel to drain. Grease from the hot frying pan spattered both the stove top and his father's wrinkled hands, but the old man didn't seem to feel it. He lifted the pan from the hot eye, then reached into the cabinet above him for plates. Harlan noticed the way the old man's shoulder blades pushed out against his shirt, like old iron plow sweeps that were filed sharp. His father's whole body looked rough and pointed, like a rusted blade.

He knew the stories about his father, how when he'd been a policeman in Demarville, he and old Mr. Arnett could "teach class on how to beat a nigger with a rubber hose." But he'd never seen any of that, and his father had never talked about it.

Harlan sat down at the table. The old man set a plate of fried eggs and bacon in front of him, then sat down with his own plate.

"You go to that nigger ballgame last night?"

"I told you I was going."

"Alfonso came by here looking for you."

"Why'd he come by? He must have known I was already gone."

"Why do they do anything? Maybe he thought he could still catch you. I don't know. Just said he had some things to tell you. Sounded all serious. You know that tone they get. Was you the only white man there?"

"Does it matter?"

"Damn right it matters. It matters one whole hell of a lot. You ought not be going to nigger places, hanging around with niggers. You been going around with them since before you quit the paper mill. Maybe you think white folks ain't good enough, that you got to shame your daddy."

The old man's elbows were set hard on the table. One hand was balled into a tight fist, the other pointing a bent finger across the table. His lips were white at the edges.

"I ain't trying to shame you. What do you want to say something like that for?"

"You're shaming yourself. Hanging out with niggers. Quitting your job. They ask you to keep your damn shoes tied and come to work with your shirt buttoned, and what do you do? Quit. All offended. Twelve years down the drain."

"I don't need the work. I've got money saved."

"Then why don't you go see folks? You hadn't gone by to see Finley and his boys in a long time. They ask about you. Go see somebody besides niggers."

Harlan got quickly up from the table, glancing down at the yellow running egg yolk, at the brittle pieces of bacon rind. He pushed his chair up to the table, then turned and walked down the hall to his bedroom and closed the door behind him.

He sat down on the ladder-back chair. A perfectly square

patch of sun shone through the east window, making the room warm. He took his shoes from beside the chair and put them on. They felt heavy, as if they were molds that had been filled with lead. His hands and arms felt just as weighted; he didn't bother to reach down and tie his laces. He could remember sitting in just this manner when he was a child. Once, he'd sat up most of the night in his room waiting for his father to come in with the strap. He'd gotten a dart set two days earlier and had made holes in the wall all around where he'd hung the board. When his father saw the holes, he'd told Harlan to count them all and not go to bed because he'd be back later with the strap to give him as many licks as there were holes. He had counted seventeen, not daring to skip any of them, but his father never came back in.

There had been a better time, he remembered—before his brother died. But that was long ago. He was thinking a lot about Barry lately. It was getting near that time of year.

Sometimes he wondered why he didn't just move out. But then he remembered when he'd lived on his own, and how it had seemed that there'd been only dead places waiting for him; houses with cold rooms.

He drove past Finley's house. Finley was standing out in his yard, beside one of the big, yellow, broken-down school buses. His hair was slicked back and he had his work clothes on. Across the road from the house, one of Finley's boys, Stephen, was working in the garden. He was dropping seeds along a row, staring carefully at the ground as he moved in a crouch.

Harlan slowed his truck, almost decided to stop, but neither of them waved; he'd only seen them a few times in the past six months. He pressed the accelerator and drove past, honking quickly and waving until he felt he'd gotten out of sight.

He drove across the highway, and down into the area of Jackson Quarter. Most of the small houses there were built with rough scrap lumber, their tin roofs rusted to a deep red. There were a few cement-block houses, painted white; brown stains marked the lower portions of the walls where rain had splashed the mud from the dirt yards. He pulled off the blacktop, pumping the brake, and drove on the hard-packed dirt. Junked cars sat in drives that were lined with worn-out tires painted white and buried halfway into the ground. In the summer flowers grew from them, but now there were only long stems of grass.

As he pulled up to Alfonso's block house, he was careful to watch out for the black children who usually ran in their games from yard to yard. There weren't any today.

By the time he got out of his truck and had leaned waiting up against the hood, Alfonso was already out of the house and walking slowly toward him. He noticed that Alfonso had on a new pair of jeans and a new shirt. The shirt was green and looked good against Alfonso's light brown skin.

"Where you going all dressed up?" Harlan asked.

Alfonso looked surprised. "I ain't going nowhere. I just got up an hour ago. What you doing?"

"What do you think I'm doing? I came by to see you. Daddy said you come by the house last night after I'd been down here looking for you."

"Wannissa told me you was looking for me. Said she seen your truck pass a heap of times."

"You knew I wanted to go to the game. Why'd you come to the house after you knew I'd be gone?"

"I don't know. Maybe I thought I could still catch you. Or maybe I thought you'd wait on your good friend, Alfonso. Your buddy. Maybe I just wanted to talk."

Alfonso's voice didn't sound normal. There was something unfamiliar, strange in the tone.

"What's wrong?" Harlan asked. "Why are you talking like that?"

"Well, a notion about you came to me lately, Harlan. Something that don't set right."

"What are you talking about?"

"You come down here hanging with me and other black folks. And that's all right, but I look at you, and I see how you don't be dressing yourself right, how you done quit your job. And you always drinking and don't never see your white friends. Then I see you with your daddy. I don't know how nobody can live with that white man, how he treats you. I figure it ain't cause you like black folks that you come down here, it's cause . . ."

"Wait a damn minute."

"It's true. I don't believe you got anything against me. But I don't know you. I'm just some somebody for to ride along with you to the ballgame. And it make me look bad."

Harlan could feel the heat of the engine rising up through the hood, the metal warm against his hands. He pushed himself away and stood up straight, rubbing his palms together. Alfonso stood still before him. It wasn't true, he thought.

"So you're saying you don't want me to come around here? Is that it?"

"Not less you do some changing about your person."

He watched Alfonso turn and walk back to his house.

He wanted to get into his truck, to go somewhere, but he just stood there and watched Alfonso's door close. He was slowly aware of the excited voices of children playing behind a nearby house. One of them squealed, sounding like some strange wild animal. Then they all laughed. For a moment he remembered playing with Barry down by the creek, both of them chasing after minnows with their bare hands and Barry letting loose a high-pitched yell every time he came close to catching one. They had been lucky if they'd caught as many as two.

He heard a higher-pitched squeal from the children behind the house, and he suddenly wished they would all shut up. He walked around to the cab and climbed in the truck.

He drove around the Loop Road twice. Cows stood in the open pastures, and the furrows of the plowed fields lay black and straight. Finally he drove to Anderson's store and pulled up to the gas pumps. The young boy, Seth, came out of the store and looked up at him.

"Same?"

"You got it."

"Ever going to up it?"

He didn't bother to answer.

Later, as he pulled into the grove of pines, he saw the old man sitting out on the steps in front of the door, staring down between his knees at the bottom step. Harlan cut the engine and sat in the truck, staring through the dirty windshield. The bright sun beating down made his father look old, but not a grandfatherly kind of oldness, he thought. The sun seemed to crack the wrinkles farther into the old man's skin. He looked like a statue—frozen, solidified in the sun's heat.

He got out of the truck and slammed the door. His father jerked up straight.

"I'm going down in the pasture to feed the calves," Harlan said.

His father looked past him. "About time," he said. "You missed the last two days. That ain't no way to do. You missed once last week too."

"I know."

Harlan walked over to the wire gap and opened it enough to squeeze through, then slipped the wire loop back over the pole. He trudged slowly through the grass to the crib and went in to where the feed was stored. Carefully he heaped two more-than-full buckets, then walked to the calf-creeper and poured the feed into the troughs. The calves were slow to come up from the bottom. Twelve finally bunched into the creeper, one shy. Maybe the other had found a hole in the fence, he thought. Maybe his patch job hadn't been strong enough. He began to walk the fence beside the road, checking the wire down the line. The bright new strands held strongly to the old. He circled back up through the pasture and walked up to where the top of a knoll was covered by a clump of oaks. He thought that maybe the calf was lying there in the shade, but it wasn't. Finally he walked up to the catch pen.

The calf was there. Not only had it gotten somehow into the pen, but it was trapped now in the narrow chute where the cows were vaccinated.

Someone had nailed the gate shut behind it, the bright heads of new twenty-penny nails glaring in the sun.

Why would someone do that? he wondered. And who?

He walked quickly up to the crib and looked through the pile of old tools. He found a nine-pound sledgehammer with a broken handle and went back down to the pen and swung the hammer against the gate. The weather-beaten boards splintered into pieces when the rusted steel struck them.

By the time he made it back to the house, the sun seemed to beat down even harder. The old man was still out on the steps.

"What the hell kept you?" he asked.

"Somebody nailed one of the calves in the chute."

"Say they did?"

"Guess I'll have to keep a better check on them," he said.

"Yeah, I guess you will at that," the old man said, looking up.

There was another game that night. He wanted to sit alone in the bleachers and watch the players move up and down the court, weaving and filling the lanes, working toward the basket. He needed to see the smooth arc of the ball as it sailed through the air and fell cleanly through the white net, touching neither board nor rim.

His father was watching the old Zenith television in the little room off the hall. He stopped beside the door and peeked in. The old man's stocking feet were resting on top of the three-legged stool before the armchair, and the large shade of the lamp blocked the rest of the old man's body from view. He knew there was a good chance his father was asleep. He hoped so. He didn't want to tell him where he was going. He thought he heard a slow and heavy exhale over the sound of the television, and he slipped past the door.

He made it to the game. He looked right at the dark-skinned man who'd been wearing the green tie, gave him his money, then walked on in and found a place down low. The score was already six to two.

☙

After finding the calf in the chute, Harlan spent most of his time out of the house, away from the old man. They would eat breakfast early, mostly in silence, then for whole mornings or afternoons he would sit at Anderson's or the Bait Shop and drink cokes or coffee, talking about anything to anyone. He ran into Alfonso once, but he didn't say much to him.

He spent the most part of two days working down in the pasture. Some boards needed replacing on the feed troughs and on the catch pen and, of course, on the vaccination chute. He walked the fence line too, putting up posted signs, but thought the place they needed putting was in the house itself.

The days began to get longer and the nights more humid. Sometimes at night there were ballgames, but lately they were more often playing out of town. The season was almost over. It wouldn't have lasted as long as it had if they hadn't made it to the state tournament.

He thought more often about Barry. At night, when he sat in the kitchen, the ceiling light burned like a heating element, seeming to warm the heavy, moist air that came in through the open door. Beetles would fly into the white globe, striking it hard enough to make the glass ring in a dull, dead way; and it would be the only sound he heard as he read the local page of the sports section, the black ink of the newsprint rubbing off on his hands, looking almost like bruises on the ends of his fingers.

"Sold." He kept hearing the word "sold" one night.

"What?" he said, looking up at the old man.

The ceiling bulb cast a hard light down on his father, but the old man's head was tilted slightly forward and the light—instead of illuminating his father's eyes—only shadowed them.

"You ain't been listening. I said I sold the place."

Harlan sat and stared past his newspaper, hoping the old man was telling an old story about some deal that had taken place a long time ago.

"Got a good price for it. Sold it to a man over in Sumter County. You'll have to sell off the cows quick. And find you a place to live."

The moist heavy air seemed to fill Harlan's chest, smothering any words he might utter. Were there even any words he could say? He stood up and looked at his father.

"You going to just stand there?"

"I thought you said it was mine now. To think of it as my own. That you were going to sign it over."

"Changed my mind. Decided I wanted the money. You don't never look after things anyway."

"Just because I miss a day of feeding . . ." He could hear the plea in his words, and he tried to control it by slowing his speech. "You know I wanted the land."

"Well, I'll do with it as I see fit. You can't expect things from me."

This was the worst. No beating or cussing had ever been as bad. He could understand a slap or hard words. Anger was simply something that had always been there inside his father. It was as natural as blood and tissue. But this he couldn't understand.

"I guess boarding up one of my calves wasn't enough for you," Harlan said softly.

The old man didn't respond.

He felt the distance between them. Looking down at his father, he remembered when the old man had given him an inexpensive set of binoculars. He and Barry had roamed all over the pasture and creek with them, scouting for Indians and outlaws. Then Barry had discovered that if they looked through the big ends of the eyepieces, the wrong ends, everything looked small and distant, even things that were close up. And now, as he looked at his father, it seemed as if he were looking through those same binoculars; the old man seemed small, far away. He felt that there was no way the old man could reach him.

He made the trips that he had to make to the stockyard. Each time he backed the trailer up to the sagging wooden gates and the ramp, and watched the cows amble out, he felt sick. And as he drove away each time from the yard he felt as empty as the trailer littered with hay and manure, as if it weren't the cows and calves he were losing, but the final parts of something he'd been losing for a long time.

The land sale was final the next week, and then there were no more games to go to. The Wildcats finally lost to a team from Tuscumbia. According to the paper they'd lost by fifteen points, and had never really been in the game. He still would have liked to have seen them play, to see if they'd had at least a trace of their sharpness left.

The days were getting even longer, and the gray dusk that hung over the pasture and the pines made him think more often of Barry. And his mother. It was the first of April; he could tell it without looking at the calendar.

On a warm Wednesday morning, two weeks before they had to be off the place, he walked into the kitchen and found the old man had already eaten and cleaned up. Dishes were draining in the rack beside the sink, and the old man looked up at him as he walked to the table.

"I've got to have the truck this morning."

"What for?"

"Got something to do and I need your truck to carry a few things. I could use the back of my car, but the truck would make it easier."

"All right," he said. Harlan handed him the key and watched him walk out the door; then Harlan went to the window and pulled back the curtain. His father was lifting a rake into the back of the truck. A few old leaves were still caught in the prongs. He was surprised that he hadn't realized what his father was going to do. He'd done it the year before and had even talked about it. And this was the week. The old man turned, walked back to the storage room, and came out with the hand clippers and two wreaths of flowers that he must have gotten in Demarville the day before. He put them in the truck and climbed into the cab. The truck lurched twice. The emergency brake had been on. After a moment the truck disappeared around the curve in the drive.

He'd been only ten when his brother died. Barry, twelve, had been diagnosed with a liver disease and although he'd lived for quite a while, it slowly took him over. Harlan remembered how horribly weak Barry became, and how when Barry wasn't in the hospital, the old man—who still patrolled nights then in Demarville—would sit with Barry during the day, doing everything for him, lifting him, cleaning him. In the evenings their mother would come in from the store, carrying in one hand a bag filled with whatever their supper was going to be, and in the other, the bag filled with the cash from the register drawer. After they ate and after the old man was practically pushed out the door, their mother would sit up with Barry. He could only go in to see his brother for a few minutes at a time before they made him leave. He remembered how Barry's body began to swell. And then when it seemed that it couldn't have swollen larger, Barry died.

Harlan hadn't understood very much about his brother's death at the time. But he did later. It was after he'd gone to look over the college in Birmingham during his senior year that he'd gotten sick. It wasn't long before they realized he had the same disease as Barry. He became weak, and then there was the time in the hospital, his body swelling slightly and his mind filling with fear. His mother hired help for the store and took almost constant care of him, but the old man was different. His father didn't help at all; he hardly seemed able to even look at him. He survived, but by the time he got through it, the scholarship was gone.

After Barry had died, April had become more than just a month in the spring of the year. It seemed to lose the new growth and greenness that made it April, and it became his mother's month. She claimed it in her expression and in the slow way she moved and talked. And April lost its boundaries of time. It began toward the end of March, when the days began to stretch out. His mother, he remembered, got home later in the evenings because she'd had to keep the store open longer. He'd waited for her outside and could tell when she would be getting home by how well he could see, and by how wet the air felt against his skin. April became a month of dusk, of that lazy slow time between day and night. After she'd gotten out of the car, she would walk over to him and, without speaking, put an arm around his shoulder and he would let her lead him into the house. Then, after she went and spoke to his father, he would follow her around in the kitchen. She moved slowly there. Often she would stand directly over the stove, staring down for a long time, and something would begin to smoke on one of the stove eyes. "Mama," he'd say, "you're letting something burn." Then she would suddenly turn and look at him with a blank, lost expression.

He remembered that his father had never acted any differently during this time. April did not seem to affect him. He was the same all year long—silent, distant, angry.

His mother's last April hadn't been very different from the others after his brother's death. It began in March. He spent a great deal of time at home with her; and although she didn't seem as far away as she once had when she spoke and worked around the house (the store had been closed for several years), there was still a sadness about her. Late in the week she and his father had driven down to Montgomery to see a couple they had once known. The man had been on the police force with his father. The old man did the driving going down, and she was driving back. Just outside of Selma they were hit by a cattle truck, and she was killed.

His father pulled into the yard a little before noon. Harlan went to the window and watched him lift the rake and clippers from the back of the truck and carry them to the storage shed. The old man moved slowly and unsteadily. A dark, narrow stain of sweat on his shirt ran from between his shoulder blades to the small of his back. He walked up the steps, opened the door, and moved past Harlan without speaking.

"You shouldn't have made yourself tired," Harlan said.

The old man kept walking down the hall. "I can still work,"

he said. "Work feels good to me—unlike some people I know."

His father seemed so tired that in the afternoon Harlan sat with him in the small room where the television was and drank a glass of iced tea while his father rested. The old man sat in the chair beside the table and lamp that Harlan's mother had bought, and Harlan sat on the sofa on the other side of the table. The lamp stood between them, and its dark shade blocked his view of his father. The only light in the room came through a half-shuttered window. He sat staring at the television screen in front of them and could see in the slightly rounded glass the reflection of the small motionless figures of himself and his father. He thought suddenly that they both looked as if they'd been cut out of cardboard and placed in front of the screen. The longer he stared the more the screen began to look like a photograph, a black-and-white photo from one of his mother's old albums, or maybe even an old tintype photo with the edges slightly bent. Each of them, it seemed to him, looked hard and brittle, caught in a distant, almost forgotten moment of time. And somewhere in the space between them there in the quiet room, the old moment seemed to still exist.

He turned and looked at his father. He couldn't see the old man's face, only his body sagging beyond the lamp between them. The old man's legs were stretched out from the chair, and his hands, folded together, rested in his lap. The skin on them was spotted with age; blue veins ran over the bones and down the length of the fingers. The nails were cut short. Both hands lay motionless; Harlan felt it was strange to see them that way. They didn't look like his father's actual hands at all, but more like a wax cast of them. It had been a long time since one of them had struck him, he thought, but he could remember clearly. He stared a little longer at the fingers, at how they were twisted by arthritis and age, and he imagined them gripping the handle of the rake as the old man had worked over the graves, pulling the rake toward him, cleaning the plot. Harlan remembered that ground when a large mound of dirt had lain beside it. He remembered sitting beside the old man listening to the preacher talk about Barry. He remembered his mother crying, and his father sitting silent with the same expression as his mother's, but without the tears.

He looked at their reflections in the dark screen again and saw the space between them, the space that had only been a moment, but had somehow become all of time and had filled his father's life. He wanted to say something to him, anything.

"You been to any nigger ballgames lately?" the old man said then.

"No, Daddy, I hadn't," Harlan said softly. He took another drink from his glass and looked again at the screen.

An Afternoon at Carter's

I T'S THAT LOOK on his face I can't forget. It keeps staying
with me, the way his eyes looked so deep and the way his
jaw was set, like he was clenching down hard on something in
his mouth. I don't mean he was sick or anything like that. His
face looked kind of like stone, but it looked like maybe it was
all soft right underneath, if that makes any sense. I'd never seen
him look that way before. Don't know if I've ever seen anybody
look that way before.

I was down there when it happened, down to Carter's house.
I go there a lot to see him and his brother, Stephen, and their
mama and daddy. I kind of feel like part of their family. You
know how you get with some people. My family's real different
from theirs, maybe that's why I like going down there.

Anyway, I was there that afternoon, and that Shetland pony was tied by the big, dead oak tree beside those poor people's house. It looked real bad. They didn't ever take care of it. Then all of a sudden the old thing busted loose from its stob, came across that broken-down fence and through the yard, and ran down between the old junk cars and the big yellow bus with all the tires flat and the beat-up furniture stored in it with the legs sticking out the windows. It ran on through the pines and over the road, and finally ended up in the garden tromping down the corn like something wild.

We were standing out in front of the house watching it, me and Carter and Stephen and their daddy. Well, I say *we* were standing. All of us were except Carter's and Stephen's daddy. He was drunk as he could be. He got up off the ground there in front of the porch and started picking up pinecones and tried to hit it with them when it ran by. Then he went to hollering and carrying on. He gets wild a lot. Stephen has to go get him out of juke joints and shot houses sometimes. Stephen don't seem to mind too much, but Carter don't ever do it. I mean ever. He hates his daddy. They're always yelling at each other. Carter even cusses him sometimes. But I like their daddy real well. He ain't nothing like mine.

Carter started to holler at his daddy. Said, "Will you just shut the hell up. You act just as crazy and stupid as that damn Shetland. You just damn like him!" Then he kind of lowered his voice, real disgusted like, and said, "Ain't got no sense."

And you know, he's partly right about his daddy. The old man does just seem to sort of bust loose sometimes, like that Shetland did, and act crazy and wild. But he's got plenty of sense.

We kept looking at it there in the garden across the road. It was stomping the squash. Then it ran through the beans like it's done about a hundred times. Their daddy says, "Somebody ought to shoot that damn pony." He said it like people say things sometimes. He didn't really mean it.

Stephen turned around, looking like he'd just lost something. "Wait a minute now, you don't say that to Carter," he said. See, Carter gets rid of stray dogs sometimes. Strays are always hanging around here. People put them out and drive away. We got one stays up at our house. Daddy beats it every once in a while, tries to run it off.

After Stephen said what he did, Carter disappeared into the house. He came back with a .22 pistol in his hand. A Smith and Wesson. You think he could have at least got a rifle. He stood there on the porch for a few minutes, just looking down at us without saying anything.

Stephen looked at his daddy. "I told you you hadn't ought to said that."

Their daddy stared at Carter up on the porch, then got quiet and leaned himself against a pine tree and sort of slid down onto the ground. He kept looking at Carter in a funny way, like maybe Carter was really as tall as he looked standing there on the porch, like he was a giant or something. Carter stared back down at his daddy and sighted that pistol dead at a pine-cone above his daddy's head. Then he came on down the steps, turned his back to his daddy, and walked on out across the road real slow, like he was fixing to fight a duel. Me and Stephen followed him. Their daddy just sat there.

I didn't know if I wanted to go at first. I got to thinking about what my old man might do to me if he found out. It would mean the belt, probably. He'd used it on me plenty of times. Carter'd seen him do it before. It embarrassed him. And me too. Anyway, I got to thinking maybe I wouldn't want to see what was about to happen, but then decided this was something I wouldn't want to miss either. I wasn't sure why.

Carter got to it before we did. The Shetland saw him and started to move on out behind the garden. It stopped right at the edge of the woods, over where Stephen was putting in a trailer. It just stood there. I don't know why it didn't keep moving. Maybe it figured it had enough distance.

We got up even with Carter, and then we all moved a little closer to the Shetland. Carter had this real serious look about him, like maybe he thought the pony was going to run him down or something.

He shot. And the pony bolted toward the trailer. Then he shot again. He hit it both times, right around the shoulder. We all ran toward it. Carter pulled up quick and raised the pistol again. The bullet must have gone right between mine and Stephen's heads. It fell this time. It's strange to see a pony drop like that.

We all went up to the pony and Carter did a funny thing. He tried to hand *me* the pistol. I don't know why. "Take it," he said. "Finish him." Like I'd want to. Like there was something between us and that this was something we should do together.

I stood there. I couldn't take the pistol. "No. I won't do it," I said. But he kept looking at me, standing there with the pistol held out. Finally I just stuck my hands in my pockets.

I'm still trying to figure out why he thought I'd want to shoot the pony too.

He shot it twice more in the head. Finished it quick. We all three stood there for a few more minutes, not saying anything, like we were waiting for a ride or something. I started thinking again what my father would do to me if he found out.

Then Stephen said, "Well, what are we going to do with it?"

"Bury it," Carter said.

"Where?" Stephen said. "At the Methodist church?"

Carter pointed behind Stephen's trailer. Said, "In that big ol' hole you got dug for the septic tank."

Stephen went around to the front of the trailer and drove back around on his backhoe. The Shetland was lying about thirty yards from the hole, and Stephen drove in behind it, put the bucket down, and started pushing the pony along the ground. Its legs flopped all over the place and its tail dragged along behind. We were all scared it was going to bust open before we got it to the hole. It had rained a lot not two days before and so when he got in close, the pony slid right along on the mud. He pushed it a little farther, and it went on over into the hole with a splash.

I never knew a pony could float. The hole was almost slap filled up with water, and the pony kind of bobbed up and down in it the way a fishing cork will do when there's a bream pulling on the line. Finally it settled and got real still and floated smooth with its back and part of its neck sticking up just above the surface. Stephen took up a scoop of dirt with the bucket and dropped it on top of the pony, and it took the pony down at first, but then the Shetland popped right back up again and bobbed around all crazy in that muddy water.

Stephen dropped a couple more scoops in, but the same thing happened each time, and at the rate things were going it looked like we were going to have the hole filled up with a pony lying on top of it. So Stephen and Carter got to arguing about what to do. Finally Stephen said, "All right, damnit. You do it." And he climbed down from the seat and Carter climbed up.

Carter said he was going to get the pony out, dip out all the water, then put the pony back in and cover him. He got that bucket down in the water and under the pony all right. Then he started trying to jerk it up out of the hole. He almost got it out several times.

While he almost had it out the fourth or fifth time, the old man walked around the trailer. He walked right to the edge of the hole without saying anything and kept looking up at Carter on the backhoe.

"Get the hell out of the way," Carter said. But his daddy didn't move.

"Get the hell out the way," he said again. The old man still didn't move. He just stood there, rubbing his hands on his pants leg.

Carter pulled the bucket out of the hole and cocked the arm back. His daddy looked down at the pony floating and bobbing in the water. You could tell he was trying not to look at Carter. Carter stared down at the old man with that same kind of look about him like right before he shot the pony. Then all of a sudden he swung that arm out wide to the right, reached the bucket out, and brought it flying around toward his daddy, stopping it just short of him. Stephen started hollering at Carter. Said, "What the hell you doing? Get your ass down from there." Their daddy didn't move. Didn't look at Carter. Nothing.

Carter pulled the bucket back around and swung it fast again. It stopped not a foot away from his daddy. Then he just kept on swinging it faster and faster, and his daddy didn't move hardly, and Stephen and me both hollered, and mud flew off the bucket, and the engine on the backhoe ran loud. The only thing that was still and quiet was the pony lying dead in the water.

Then it hit. I couldn't believe it at first. Carter had swung so close so many times. We all watched his daddy go down into the hole. Seemed like he dropped just like that pony did. I think it took Carter longer to believe it than it took for me and Stephen. He drew the bucket back and stared at where his daddy had been standing.

Me and Stephen ran up to the hole. The pony and their daddy were bobbing all crazy-like. The pony's legs were coming up out of the water, and their daddy couldn't use but one arm to try and get out. Me and Stephen sprawled ourselves flat on the ground in the mud and reached for him. I grabbed his hand once, but couldn't hang on.

Next thing I know, Carter's right between me and Stephen, and he grabbed hold of his daddy's arm and pushed Stephen out of the way. He started pulling his daddy up, and that's when I saw it. That's when I saw that look on Carter's face. I just can't quit thinking about it. His eyes looked so deep. He wasn't crying like you see some people cry, but he was crying like a man will when you can't see any tears. His nostrils were quivering and his jaw was tight and you could see the veins in his neck pumping. He looked down at his daddy and his face . . . well, it looked full of something. He had a look on him like somebody might want to draw, but wouldn't ever get right.

Carter got the old man out of the hole, and they took him to Demarville to the hospital. His arm was broken and three of his ribs were cracked.

That afternoon I walked home, by myself. When I got a little ways from the house I saw my old man sitting outside on the porch all rigid in a straight-backed chair. He looked like something. When I got close he jumped up and hollered at me like a sergeant. Said, "Where the hell you been? Don't you have enough damn sense to stay out of the mud? Are you stupid?"

I looked at him standing up there on the porch, and he stared down at me. I wouldn't answer him. All I could think about was how that bucket swung hard and fast.

The next day Stephen finished burying the pony. He had to do it by himself. Carter sat out on the porch with his daddy shelling peas in a pan. They rang against the metal like loose birdshot.

Accusations

HIS FATHER HAD just picked him up at the station in Demarville; they were headed home. He'd been in Montgomery again, seeing his mother. The warm wind filled the inside of the car with heat and moisture, but even the humid air felt good to Seth after having ridden on the bus for three hours. He'd stayed at his mother's for two weeks this time. He liked it there. He could drink a beer or let a "hell" or a "damn" slip and it was all right. And she stayed out of his way. But now that he was with his father . . .

The two lanes of asphalt shot straight out in front of them through the low, flat land between the Tennahpush and Black Fork rivers. The road was built up on a high bank overrun with kudzu, and the backwater from both rivers ran along either side. The water, full of turtles and snakes, reminded Seth of the mud-yellow creek that ran slowly through his grandfather's pasture. He hadn't walked along its banks in months; he thought that he would go down there in the next day or so and see if he could find a cottonmouth to shoot. After all, it would be his last summer before going off to college. He wanted to spend some time out of doors, roaming the pasture and woods.

Just after they'd passed three black women fishing off the roadbank, his father told him the news.

"Erin's pulled another one. She's walked off her job in Yellowstone."

He heard the familiar tone of disapproval that his father used when talking about Erin.

"Kate doesn't know where she is. All she could find out over the phone is that Erin and two other girls quit at the same time and headed for California. They left two and a half weeks ago. Kate hasn't heard a word."

Seth thought that his stepsister would probably be all right. She always was.

"Kate's called the highway patrol out there. She's almost frantic. I've tried to reassure her and keep her calm. I'm sure Erin'll finally call. She just doesn't stop to think about anybody else. Inconsiderate thing."

His father bore down on the accelerator and passed a slow-moving truck. "You're a good boy," his father said then. "A good son. The best any father could hope for."

Seth had heard this so many times he expected it. He turned toward his window and watched the black creosote fence posts flash past.

After stopping at his grandfather's store to say hello and to get gas for the car, they drove home. He headed straight to his bedroom first thing; he wanted to unpack and put away his clothes. And he really didn't want to face his stepmother right away, not after the news his father had just told him. He didn't know what kind of state he'd find her in. He took his time hanging his shirts and even refolded his blue jeans before he put them away.

When he finally went in to see her, she was sitting on the sofa in the living room, leaning forward. A book lay open on her lap. It was a Bible—his Bible, he thought. The church had given all the high school students in the congregation Bibles with their names printed in gold on the front. He'd never read his. One day he saw her reading it, marking in it, not long after Erin had said that there was no way she'd ever finish school and had then come in drunk or stoned the next morning after staying out all night. He'd been glad that someone was using the Bible. But he'd wished she had at least asked him for it.

His father was sitting beside her on the sofa. Her voice sounded quiet and frail, like someone confessing a sin in a confessional booth, the way he'd seen it on television, anyway. His father nodded as she spoke.

When Seth walked farther into the room, he heard her say something about the highway patrol, that either they had called or that she'd called them again. She glanced up at him; his father turned suddenly.

"Is your bedroom cool enough?" he said. "I opened the vents in there this morning."

He wished his father wouldn't interrupt her like that.

"Hey, Kate," he said. Then, "My room's fine."

"Well good," his father said.

"Conrad, I was telling you I called again," his stepmother said.

"I know. I'm listening."

"I don't think you were. I said they didn't know anything. And didn't sound like they'd be much help." She closed the Bible and clutched it tightly.

"She'll be all right. She'll call soon, and in the meantime we're doing all we can," his father said. "I'll call tomorrow."

"How's your mother, Seth?" Kate asked, then looked past him, out into the hall.

"She's fine."

"Good."

"Kate, I'm sure you'll hear from Erin," he said.

"Your grandmother called a few minutes ago. She says she's fixing you a supper just like you like," his father said.

He knew that meant fried chicken.

"That sounds good. I think I'll go on over there pretty soon."

"I'll take you."

"I'd like to walk through the pasture."

"Let me take you."

He went back to his room and put on a different pair of shoes. After a few minutes he heard his father's footsteps. He'd wondered how long it would take before his father followed him. The door opened wide.

"Are you about ready to go?"

He looked at his father, noticing that he seemed a little tired; his shoulders weren't held as straight as usual.

"Yes. I'll maybe go down in the pasture tomorrow."

"I'd really like to go down to your grandparents for a while, too. But I guess I'd better not stay long," he said, looking back to the front of the house where Kate was.

When they walked outside he noticed that the sun sat on the

treetops now and that the air felt slightly cooler than it had been. He thought of his grandmother's meal and of stretching out on his grandparent's floor, listening to them talk about the day's business, about who'd come into the store, and what news they'd heard. He could always relax there.

He didn't know what time it was. The alarm clock wasn't working, but the sun shone bright through his curtains. He thought that it was at least mid-morning, maybe ten o'clock. He stretched his arms and then propped his head up on the two pillows, debating about how much longer he should lie in bed.

Then he heard the sound. Hard footsteps. He not only heard them, he felt the hardwood floors of the old house shake. He shut his eyes and bowed his head, anticipating. Something inside himself seemed to break loose and then sink into his stomach. It couldn't be happening again, he thought. Not after all this time. But he knew that it was.

The pounding moved on through Erin's vacant room and into the bathroom; then he heard what he knew could only be a fist beating against the other side of the bathroom door. Even as the muscles up and down his body tensed, he noticed the distinct hollow sound the fist made against the door, the thin sheets of plywood almost like skins on a drum.

"Seth! Are you up? I'm going to open this door right now," she said.

"All right."

The door opened and she stepped past the threshold. She wore an old blue housecoat buttoned all the way to her neck. Her eyes bulged slightly.

"Two of my rings are missing! I've looked all over. I saw

them both just last week. One belonged to my great-grand-mother. I want to know what you've done with them. I want to know right now."

He breathed evenly, trying to stay calm.

"I don't have your rings, Kate."

"You're lying! I forgave you for those other times. Forgave you in my heart."

He clenched his hands into fists underneath the sheet. The idea of her forgiving him for something he'd never done was more than he could bear. He sat suddenly upright in bed. "I don't have your rings! I've never stolen anything from you." He was startled by the force behind his words. He'd never spoken to her as strongly.

"You're not who everybody thinks you are," she said. "And there's one person who sure doesn't know. You know who I mean."

She kept staring at him, getting more red in the face. He felt that she hated him.

"Don't you be telling your daddy about this. This is between me and you. Leave him out of it. Just get those rings back to me by this afternoon."

"I don't have your rings. When have I even had the chance to go into your room and take them?"

She stepped back into the bathroom and placed her right hand on the doorjamb.

"No, you're not who everybody thinks you are. But I know. You're no saint."

She shut the door. The floor shook slightly as the sound of her footsteps receded into Erin's room.

Her last words stayed with him. They somehow made him

feel as if he had done something wrong, had committed some crime that he couldn't quite remember.

He lay back on his bed. He felt tired, as if he'd just loaded fifty-pound sacks of horse feed into someone's pickup at the store. But his hands were still closed into fists, and he clenched them tight again. He decided that he didn't care what she'd said about telling his father. He knew that she was only trying to protect herself.

The pool lay still, like rainwater collected in a wooden barrel. Just before lunch he'd slipped out of the house, and now he searched the banks and sandbars for any movement, looked for any ripple on the water's surface. Sometimes moccasins raised their arrow-shaped heads and quietly broke the water. He had his .22; the rifle had been his grandfather's, and his father's. It was small, really only a boy's gun, but it was the one he always carried to the creek.

Briars grew thick along the edges of the banks. He picked his way through them carefully, but they ripped at his legs through his jeans. Tree limbs reached out over the water; and, despite the shade, he could see small bream in the shallows. He watched them dart from one bed to another, then into the deeper part where he couldn't see them. Then suddenly they were back over the beds, fanning their tails.

It had been ten dollars once—the second time. She'd stomped into the living room where he'd been watching television. "Ten dollars is missing," she said. "I hid ten dollars in Erin's room, and now it's gone. Erin says she didn't even know it was in there."

He didn't know what he was supposed to say. He wasn't

even sure if he was being accused. He could think only, Why would she hide money in Erin's room?

Then his father came in from the kitchen. "What are you implying?" he said. His voice was deeper than usual.

She turned and looked at him, and to Seth's surprise, her hard expression remained.

"Ten dollars is missing!" she repeated.

"What are you trying to say?"

She looked at both of them, then was silent for a moment.

"I'm not trying to say anything. But ten dollars is missing and it didn't just get up and walk away."

"What's happened is obvious," his father said. "Erin took the money and lied to you when you asked her about it."

With this she turned and walked out, shaking the floors with each hard step.

The first time she'd done it had been during the early months of their marriage, when he'd been fourteen. That June they'd moved into their house, the old family place, where his father and grandfather had been born—both of them in what became Erin's room. This was following the two years that he and his father had lived with his grandparents after the divorce and the move from Montgomery.

He'd been asleep on a Sunday morning and there had been the pounding noise, then the door being jerked open. He'd been afraid for a moment that someone, his father maybe, had been hurt, that he needed to be rushed to the hospital in Valhia or Demarville.

A watch. She told him he'd stolen a gold watch. The same kind of look was on her face as when he'd once come home, opened the kitchen door, and found her pointing a .22 pistol in his face. She'd heard him in the house and thought someone had broken in. He hadn't been able to decide then how much of her expression had shown anger and how much fear. He was more successful in reading her face as she stood over him and accused him of stealing the watch. She seemed so sure of herself he almost wondered if he had taken it, and forgotten.

"I didn't steal it," he said flatly.

His father came in and heard her accusing him. He took her into the front of the house. Fifteen minutes later she came back and apologized, looking at the floor while she spoke.

His legs began to stiffen now, and he realized he'd been standing still, staring at the water. He shifted the rifle into the crook of his left arm and continued up the creek, searching each pool. He noticed that the far bank of the best and deepest fishing hole—the one in the horseshoe bend—had cracked and broken off into the water, leaving exposed the roots of a large oak tree.

Finally he came to the hole at the end of the fence line. He propped the rifle carefully up against a tree, then sat down and began to throw flat rocks into the pool, watching the ripples run over the water in their perfect widening circles. He listened to the cars pass on the nearby road. Then he pulled up a blade of grass, held it between his thumbs, and blew on it. The noise was shrill, but not loud.

He stood after a while, picked up his .22, and fired one quick shot into the muddy, slow-moving water.

Two cars were parked at the gas pumps. He walked past them, then along the side of the store building. He opened the door where the trucks came to unload and stepped into the cement-block store. The damp smell of sweeping compound came up to meet him.

He found his grandfather slicing a side of bacon and asked where his father had gone.

"I ain't seen him. Maybe he went to town, to Demarville," his grandfather said.

His grandmother, May, called from behind a showcase. She was counting cookies for a black child. "I haven't seen him either," she said as she dropped a final cookie into the small paper bag.

"Well, I was hoping he might be up here. I've got something I wanted to tell him about."

Both of his grandparents looked at him for a moment without saying anything. Then his grandfather said only, "Uh-oh," blinked his eyes hard twice and went back to slicing bacon.

He walked home past the graveyard and the red-brick Methodist church. Kate's car sat in the drive again. She hadn't been home when he'd come in from the pasture. He'd been glad. Now his insides tightened as he walked up onto the porch and opened the front door.

"It's me," he called, as he always felt he had to when she was home alone, so that he wouldn't open a door or turn a corner and find a pistol aimed at his head.

She didn't answer. Her bedroom door was closed, but he knew she had to have heard him.

He went to his room and lay down on the bed. Bright light poured through the window, and he gazed at the shadows of the window's crosspieces outlined perfectly on the hardwood floor.

Later he ventured into the kitchen. He made a ham sandwich and sat at the table eating, trying to understand why she did the things she did; why, for a third time now, she had become that other person—the one who had lived in the back of his mind since that first time.

He heard her open the bedroom door, then sit down on an old chair in the hall and pick up the phone. He heard her voice; it was weak.

"Her first name's Erin," he heard her say. He knew her calling out there was of no use.

There were pauses in the conversation. He guessed that they switched her from one officer to another. She said finally, "Well, all right then," and hung up.

He stood from the table and walked quietly out the kitchen's front entrance and onto the long porch. He ran Erin's dog off the steps and watched a few cars pass along the road. Someone was cutting the churchyard with a riding mower. Its blade kept throwing out rocks. He could hear the thin piece of metal striking them.

After what he felt was a long enough wait, he went back inside. But as he came through the kitchen, he heard her. By the time he figured out what she was saying, it was too late to turn around—he was already in the living room.

"Bring back my daughter, please," he heard. "Don't let anything happen to her. There's so much I need to say to her, to make her understand. I know I'm responsible. I didn't teach her better, wasn't the mother I should have been. It's my fault. Bring her back, please. She's all . . . it's my fault."

She was on her knees in front of the sofa; her hands were clasped together over his Bible, and she leaned over it as far as she could reach. She looked as if she were outside in a pouring rain, trying to protect the thin, holy pages. He thought of the way a mother might hover over a child to protect it.

He stared at her. He couldn't help himself. Her head was bowed deeply, and he saw how white the back of her neck looked, how frail the bones were there. The muscles in the side of her face were pulled tight, the jaw clenched. He no longer sensed hate. Her sadness and worry seemed as deep to him now as her anger had seemed that morning.

He took another step, and she jerked her head up at him and came up from her knees.

"You scared me to death! Why do you always do that?" Her eyes were pinched closed, as if swollen. "How can you just stand there and watch someone in prayer? That's almost wicked."

"I'm sorry," he said. "I didn't mean to startle you. Why would I want to?"

Before she spoke again he walked quickly out of the living room and to the back of the house, slamming the door to his room behind him.

As he lay on his bed, he kept picturing her with the Bible, hovering over it as if it were a child. He thought then of something Erin had once told him—told him half out of spite. She'd said that she had tried to leave once, but her mother hadn't let her go.

"She was all over me," Erin had said. "Grabbing me, hugging me. I begged Mama. I said, 'I don't want to stay here. I hate this redneck place. I want to live with my father.' She kept hovering over me and squeezing me. Then she started begging. She said, 'Don't go. I need you to stay. If you'll just tell me what I can do, I'll do better.' She almost knocked us both down, and she kept saying it was her fault." Erin had laughed then. "I didn't know what she was talking about."

He stood now by his window. The sun had lowered and wasn't as strong through the glass as it had been. He recalled Erin's final words. "They hadn't been married but two months at the time, that was all. But I already wanted out of here."

He slowly ran his hands over the window panes. Two months. That was all. He nodded his head then, as if to say the word "yes" into the silent room while he remembered the first time she'd stormed in and accused him; they had only been married a few months when she'd done it. And now, this third time, Erin had just hurt her mother again. Things made sense, finally.

Fault. That was the word that ran now through his mind. Kate had used the word so many times, had said that she was at fault. He'd heard the guilt she felt in her voice. But somehow he felt guilty, too, felt again as if he had stolen the rings. What was his fault? What had he done wrong? Was it simply that he was there for her to take her anger out on him, or was it because he was the "good son," seldom in any trouble, never speaking out, "perfect" in the eyes of his father? Was this what he was guilty of? He didn't feel like the perfect son, but he hadn't done anything to change his father's perception. He didn't usually let his anger show, didn't do such things as stay out all night. But there were things that he did do. He did drink, sneak in bars. He did get angry. He felt anger now, but he wasn't sure why. Had he somehow lied about himself, he wondered. Who was at fault here? Kate? Erin? Himself? His father? He didn't know. Maybe all of them. Maybe none.

Later his father came home. He heard the car door slam, then the front door, and then he heard his father's footsteps—solid and even—as he made his way to the back bedroom.

He knocked.

"Come on in. It's open," Seth said.

He sat up on his bed and leaned his back against the wall, waiting to see his father's face come around the open door.

"Hey," his father said, now standing in the room. "I had to stay in town longer than I thought. I wanted to spend the time with you. What've you been doing with yourself?"

"I went down to the pasture for a while," he said. "Then I went to the store a few minutes."

"Did you see anything at the creek?"

"No."

"Not even a turtle?"

"I thought I might spend the night down at Grandmama and Granddaddy's," he said, suddenly, then looked out the window. He could feel his father watch him.

"Anything wrong?"

"No. Nothing's wrong."

"Well, I'm sure they'd like to have you down there. I'm glad to see you thinking about your grandparents. You're a good son."

Seth closed his eyes, took a deep breath, then opened them. He still looked out the window.

"Daddy, don't say that. I'm not any better than anybody else."

"Well, to me you are. You're the best son any father could hope for."

He let out the breath that he found he'd been holding. The air went out of his lungs, and his body felt as if it were contracting like a balloon that someone might be holding open.

Longer Than Summer

THE FIRST TIME I saw Jimmy Neal and stared into those blue water-color eyes of his and saw that sweet red mouth like a little boy's was right after school let out for the summer. I was down at the Bait Shop and spotted him in front of the counter. I walked over real quick and got a Coke out of the box, then made my way straight to the cash register and cut right in front of him. I didn't even know his name then, but I knew he wouldn't say anything, knew he'd be too bashful to say how rude I was. I could tell it just by looking at him. But he wasn't so bashful that he didn't take notice of my shape. Grown men look at me. I don't always know if I like it or not, but they look.

I paid for my Coke and went over and plopped down in a chair by the door, then raised the bottle up. Jimmy Neal finally came walking by. He had a Dr. Pepper in his hand and a sweet roll. Then I said the dumbest thing. "You look hot," I said.

"Yeah, I reckon so," he said and looked at how his shirt was stuck to his chest with sweat. Then we just kind of looked at each other, embarrassed. The work crew with him started staring at us, and I felt like my top had come unbuttoned.

I finally got something else out. "You with the people putting in the water system?"

"Yeah," he said, then studied his feet. "It's Daddy's company. We're going to be here most of the summer. Well maybe. I mean me. I mean I'll be here most of the summer. The others might be longer."

He turned red then. That light skin of his caught fire, and he started rubbing his face and neck with one hand. I could feel myself getting nervous. I get nervous around people, especially guys.

"Where y'all going to be staying?" I said.

"We got a trailer down at The Landing. That's where we're staying at. At The Landing." He went to rubbing his face hard then.

He was so nervous. Lot more than me. It was sweet. But I liked it for another reason. It was like he wasn't as strong as me. I knew more, was in charge you might say.

He looked like he was about to bolt right out the door then. "I'll be seeing you," I said and looked into those pale eyes of his. He looked into mine, then was gone like a shot from a gun.

If I had known what all was going to happen, I would've stayed home, would've never wanted to meet Jimmy Neal. But maybe that's a lie. Sooner or later I would have met him, and it would've all happened. Some things are going to happen no matter what you do, and besides, Jimmy Neal didn't bring any of it on. He didn't have anything to do with what our daddies did. He was just there, standing sweaty and dirty and rumpled in the Bait Shop, where I saw him and picked him like he was some kind of a prize off the shelf at a carnival, a stuffed bear or a box of candy. I didn't even know what a prize he really was or what he could give me. I just wanted something different. If only I'd had enough sense to know what I really wanted. Anyway, when I found out that he was going to be here just for the summer, like he was sent to me, I knew then that this boy was going to be my summer.

So I started going to the Bait Shop, hoping I'd run into Jimmy Neal again. There was work for me to do at home. A lot. I wouldn't do it. For one thing, Mama wanted me out in the garden with her, hoeing. She needed help, and she likes for us to do stuff together. I used to like it too, when I was little. I'd help her wash the dishes. Daddy would dry, sometimes. For some reason I don't like to be around Mama much anymore. I'm hateful, I guess. We don't do the dishes together, and the three of us hardly ever eat at the table. Daddy almost never does. He doesn't help with anything. And he never pays much attention to anyone, especially me. He looks at me like I'm that old wrecked piece of truck out there in the yard that doesn't run and can't be fixed.

Mama's not like that. Sometimes when we're watching the television she gets up and hugs me, but I get tense and hard, turn into iron. She can feel it. It's like she wants something from me that I used to have when I was little but don't have anymore. There's a hurt look in her eyes when she pulls back. I don't know how to act with her anymore. I always turn away from her, look toward Daddy, like I'll find something there.

She looks at Daddy the same way. She wants the same thing from him as I do. She'll get up and go to bed, ask Daddy if he's coming too, but he'll say, "No, I'm going to stay up a while," and then go back to cleaning his gun, or whatever, as usual. There will be that hurt look in her eyes, and I'll want to kill him, but I'll remember then that she's looked at me the same way. She'll go on to bed, not let on that she's hurt. She'll say "good night," real cheerful, hug me. Then it's just me and Daddy, sitting in the den together. We don't say anything, just sit there. Me and him. Strange, but that's when I feel almost close to him. It's then that I feel most like his daughter.

It didn't take me long to get things started with Jimmy Neal. He was at the Bait Shop again after a few days, covered with mud from where he'd been down in a ditch. I think he didn't want me seeing him look that dirty. There was even mud on his face, but his eyes looked so clean and pure, peering out from all that black mud. The way he kept looking down at his feet, something kind of gave way inside of me, dropped down in my stomach, just for a second. It hurt almost.

"I might come swimming down at The Landing one evening," I said. It was the first thing to come to mind and it was all wrong. "Maybe you'd like to come out and swim too?"

"I don't know," he said, shaking his head.

"I just thought you might want somebody to talk to."

"That would be all right," he said.

He didn't want to go swimming, and I knew why.

Daddy wasn't home late that next afternoon, which was good, because sometimes he won't let me have the car. Doesn't give me any reason. I told Mama I wanted to go into town and look at new bathing suits. Of course that's not where I went. I don't know why I lied.

There were a good many campers and tents down at The Landing, and there was no telling which camper was Jimmy Neal's and his daddy's, so I just parked by the water, hoping he'd see me, and pulled my jeans and shirt off in the car. My bathing suit was underneath, a red and white one-piece. It looks good.

I got out and looked around for Jimmy Neal, hoping he'd come before I had to get in the water. See, no one ever swims here. Not anybody. But I figured Jimmy Neal didn't know that when I talked to him. Weeds grow all along the bank and on out into the muddy water. It looks snaky. And because of the boats putting in and out, gas and oil slicks lie on the water, stain the river a sick-looking blue. Fish heads lie on the bank, where flies and stray cats get at them. The smell can be pretty tough sometimes, like a dump.

I waited awhile for Jimmy Neal, then finally took a breath and stepped on down the cement ramp. That water sure felt cold, and I walked slow and careful. There's broken glass all around. The fishermen throw their beer bottles and bust them against the banks, and the ramp too. I didn't want to cut myself open, but I kept walking on out, hoping all the while that Jimmy Neal would come up. A breeze raked across my skin, and the water, cold, rose up my legs and to my thighs. No other girl in Riverfield would do what I was doing. Not one of them would come down here to this boat landing at almost dark and swim by herself in the Tennahpush, not for any reason. Not because they wanted someone. They talk about the way I have guys, like I buy them, or steal them, or something. But I don't do all they say.

I felt strong, like I wanted to break something, then noticed how the water lay smooth, like old dark glass. I dove against it, almost afraid it would hurt. When I was under I tasted mud. It was bitter, like paregoric, but the water felt good. Sometimes a warm current would wrap itself around me like a blanket, then be gone.

It started getting dark and everything sounded a long way off, car doors slamming, people laughing, having a good time. I thought about home for a minute, what Mama and Daddy would be doing. If Daddy was home yet. It got real quiet and the laughing all stopped. I crossed my arms against my breasts and grabbed my shoulders, the way someone will when they're cold or maybe alone at the picture show.

Jimmy Neal called "Carrie" from the bank then. His voice sounded so good. He must have thought that anyone would have to be crazy to go out in that water, but he never let on. I swam in and walked up the ramp with the water dripping off me. That musty river smell stayed on my skin and I felt dirty. He stood way up on the bank and looked out over the water, like he was waiting for somebody else to come swimming up from out of the river. When I got almost to the top of the ramp I stepped on a rock and my foot turned a little, so I just went ahead and practically fell down, even let out a little holler. He came down off the bank then. "Did you sprain your ankle?" he said. I told him I believed so.

He let me put my arm around his neck, and I limped up to the artesian well, leaning on him pretty heavy. He was strong. I kept telling myself, "It's the right foot. The right." When we got to the well, he held my foot under the water flow. He said the cold water would help keep the swelling down. Then he told me to hold it where it was, that he'd be back in a minute.

He wasn't gone long, and he came back with a plastic bag full of ice. He held my foot in his lap and put the ice on my ankle. It was cold, but his hands were strong and felt good. Mama and Daddy used to doctor on me when I was little and would hurt myself, and I felt like a little girl again for a minute. Then I remembered what I was doing.

He held the ice on me for a long time. It had turned good dark, but there was a light by the well that had come on. We were both quiet. I knew he would be, but I couldn't think of anything to say. I was nervous and just let him hold my foot. After a while he looked at the ankle. "You must have only twisted it," he said. "I don't think it's swelled at all." But he kept holding it and looking at me. The light above us made his blond hair shine, and I couldn't help but think what an angel he was. He was so sweet and trying to be good to me, and there I was, fooling him. I got up then on my left leg. I couldn't have stayed any longer.

"I got to get home," I said. He looked disappointed.

We sat out on the picnic table in front of their camper the next afternoon. I had shorts on and caught Jimmy Neal looking at my legs once or twice. Then his daddy came out and looked me over. He was real tall and had big hands. His daddy didn't make any bones about it. He looked right at my legs and then said, "Nice to meet you," to my thighs. It didn't seem like Jimmy Neal could be his daddy's son. The two of them didn't match. I'd already been hearing rumors about his daddy slipping around with a certain blonde woman, one who most people don't think too much of, especially the other women around here. His daddy seemed all wrong for him, and it made me wonder if we all get a wrong daddy.

Jimmy Neal and me took a walk through the woods down by the water. A barge with the name *Mobile Queen* on the side pushed by us loaded with coal. It made the water slap at the bank. Finally we sat down on a log, an old oak tree. He kept looking out across the water like he might see another barge. I waited, but knew it would take him forever, so I went ahead and pulled him close, kissed him the way a man should kiss a woman. He put his arms around me, held me. That was all. Didn't say a word. Not what most guys would do. I kissed him again, ran my fingers through his hair. It felt soft and fine. A little daylight was still left, and I could see right into his water-color eyes. His lashes grew so long. I envied them. Envied his hair, even his smooth skin.

When I got home, Daddy was sitting in the living room by himself, staring at the blank television, like if he looked at it hard enough it would come on and there would be something on it he'd want to see, or maybe it was more like he didn't even know he was in the living room, or at least was wishing he was somewhere else. Seems like he's always somewhere else. I don't know why. I wonder if it's me somehow. Feel like I must have done something. Or maybe it's just my very presence that bugs him.

"I just got back from taking a little drive," I finally said. He looked at me like I'd just told him I'd committed a crime, like I must have run over someone. He didn't say anything. He only cut the television on. There was just the news. A war was going on somewhere, people shooting at each other. I went on to my room and sat on the bed and thought about Jimmy Neal. I didn't figure Daddy would like him. He'd say Jimmy Neal wasn't from around here, that he worked with scummy people.

&

Something started happening between Mama and Daddy on into the summer, when the days started getting longer and even hotter. Daddy hasn't ever talked much, but he was even quieter than usual when he'd come home, hulking through the front door. He stopped yelling at me so all of a sudden and seemed like he just went to completely ignoring me. More and more Mama started going to bed without him. Of course Daddy works different shifts. Sometimes he sleeps half the day, goes in late at night. I've spent half my life tipping around the house so as not to bother him. Mama has too.

I asked Mama if anything was wrong with her and Daddy. She was folding a sheet and stopped, said, "Why, no." She concentrated on the sheet corners in her hands. "Your father's just the way he is," she said and started folding the sheet again, but she couldn't get the right corners together. "That's the way some men are, like they're someplace else. He's just got things on his mind," she said.

"Money?" I said.

"No, that's not it." She looked down at the floor then.

After that I stayed busy with Jimmy Neal most of the time and tried not to think too much about Mama and Daddy. When he'd get off work for the day he'd want me to come down to The Landing. We'd walk along the river or cook hamburgers out on the grill. I got bored with that pretty quick though. I wanted more excitement.

At night after we'd all eat out on the picnic table, his daddy would go into the trailer, then come back out all cleaned up, his hair combed back. He'd drive off then. There were even more rumors about him and that woman, and I figured the things people said about him were true enough. But I didn't know then how much there was to it, how complicated it would all get. The secrets some people keep.

On Saturdays and Sundays I'd make Jimmy Neal take me to the sandbar out on the river. That's where everybody goes to swim and ski. The sand's white and clean, and when the sun beats down on it you feel like you're at the Gulf, almost. Jimmy Neal didn't really like going. Once he even said, "No. Not this time." It surprised me. But I talked him into it. I wanted to see my friends there, and all the girls would wonder where Jimmy Neal came from. He was kind of a mystery to them, and I made sure they all knew we were together. I'd put my arm around him or hold his hand. It embarrassed him, being paraded around like that. I showed him off, like maybe if I'd wanted to I could have made him do tricks too, stand on his head, walk on his hands, like he was there to do whatever I wanted. He should have slapped me.

One night after his daddy left, we drove up to the Bait Shop. It was so hot out we needed something cold to drink, something that would taste good. He parked his truck and went inside. It took him awhile. I wish now I'd gone inside with him.

First thing that happened was Lamar. He's this guy I know, or used to know, and he was there by my window all of a sudden. I didn't see him drive up or anything. He was so close up on me I could smell his breath. There wasn't whiskey on it. It was just bad, like sour milk. "You been seeing that boy inside," he said. His voice scared me. It's not that he talks loud. His voice is kind of low and quiet, like he means something ugly. He can ask you if you want to go to the store with him and you think of his back seat.

"What's his name?" he wanted to know.

"Jimmy Neal," I said. I didn't want to talk to him. Not at all. He's kind of mean, squinty-eyed. He hit me once, gave me a black eye when I wouldn't do something he thought I ought to go ahead and do. Said he didn't mean to, that it was an accident. Daddy found out who hit me and went and had a talk with Lamar. I screamed at him not to do it, to leave Lamar alone, but he went anyway and deep down I loved him for it. Lamar didn't bother me anymore, not till now.

"I ain't seen you around much," he said. "I thought sure I'd see you this summer, but it's been weeks now. Thought this would be your summer. Thought maybe I'd be the one to make it that way."

"What are you talking about?" I said.

He laughed. "You know what I'm talking about."

I just turned away from him, pushed myself farther away from the door.

"You ain't been coming up off that stuff have you, that stuff you wouldn't never let me have? Do everything but that, wouldn't you?"

"Go to hell," I said. "Jimmy Neal's not like you are."

"You ain't nothing but a tease. Somebody ought to rape you."

I stared straight out the window shield. Didn't move, didn't say anything. I felt sick inside, like there was rust in my stomach from a hard iron thing. Right then I hated Lamar, and hated myself too. Lamar laughed and walked off.

So there I sat. About the time Lamar reached for the door a set of headlights shined against the side of the Bait Shop. It was Daddy's truck. He got out, looked at me, then toward Lamar. He didn't come over and say anything to me and didn't say a word to Lamar, just looked at him. Daddy went on inside and spoke to Jimmy Neal. I could see them through the window. Mama must have told him about us after I'd finally told her. Lamar didn't go inside, just stood by the door. Then he got in a car with somebody and they drove off.

All of a sudden it hit me that Daddy was supposed to be working a double shift. He has to sometimes, and Mama had said he was that night. I couldn't figure out why he wouldn't be at work and started to go in and ask him what had happened, but then I thought, Why bother? He won't hardly tell me what he's doing anyway. I'm glad that I didn't go in after him. He didn't come home until in the morning.

Jimmy Neal came out finally and handed me my Coke. He said he was sorry it took him so long and kissed me on the cheek. His lips felt cold. I didn't tell him about Lamar, or that Daddy was supposed to be at work. In fact, I didn't say much the rest of the night, not when we were back down on the Tennahpush or even when he took me home. I was quiet, like him. No, that's not right. I was quiet like Daddy's quiet. He asked me what was wrong. I told him "nothing." And when he tried to kiss me again back down on the river, I just sat there like a statue. I don't know why. "Tell me what's wrong," he said. "Don't just tell me 'nothing.'" He was mad. I remember looking at him, wondering what in the world I was doing. I wanted him for some reason, wanted something from him. I kept thinking about Lamar and what he said—his sour words —and the things I used to do with him. I knew what Lamar's back seat looked like. A barge came along the Tennahpush then. It's cold spotlight hit the water, ran along the banks. I felt like that barge—slipping past everything in the dark.

∞

177

I didn't go see Jimmy Neal for a few days. Didn't do much of anything. Mama got me out in the garden one afternoon, though. The work felt good, even though the hoe handle rubbed blisters on my hands. I never did tell her about seeing Daddy. Didn't want to think about it, or anything else for that matter, not Jimmy Neal, not Daddy.

Later Daddy came home and glanced at me lying on the sofa. "Is this the shift you're going to be working for a while?" I said.

He looked out the window at something or other, studied whatever it was real hard. "Yeah," he said, then walked on past me.

In a minute he came back in the room, looked at me like he just now knew I was inside. He'd taken off his work shirt, was standing there in his white T-shirt and dirty khaki pants.

"Why do you need to know what shift I'm working?"

"Just curious," I said.

He looked out the window again and back at me, stared me right in the face, then walked on out.

Mama came in from outside and went back to the bedroom where Daddy was and shut the door. They started talking and their voices got loud. I cut on the television and watched some dumb movie with cowboys and Indians. Nothing else was on.

Their door opened after a while and Daddy came out, sat in his chair, and studied the television. We didn't say a word, just watched together. I wanted to say something to him, but didn't know what. So finally I said something dumb, like I did with Jimmy Neal. "Not much good is it?" I said.

"No, not really."

"Ain't that the way it always is. You sit down wanting to watch television and nothing good's on?"

He laughed, barely, said, "Yeah, that's kind of the way it is."

178

You wouldn't ever think it, but he's got a good laugh, real deep. I've heard it when he's talking with other men about people he works with or knows around the county, but I've never heard it too much around the house.

Mama came in. She gave Daddy a hard look, and then, for some reason, gave me one too. Daddy looked down at his hands and studied his knuckles. I took a look at my hands too, noticed my nails were getting long. Mama walked right up to Daddy, stood over his chair. Her eyes were puffy and her hands shook a little, like she was a sick old woman, only in the face she looked strong as she could be. "You come back to that room right now," she said.

He looked up at her, then glanced at me for a second. He had a pleading look in his eyes, and I wanted all of a sudden to tell Mama to leave him alone.

They went back to the bedroom and shut the door. Mama started hollering then, something she *never* does. His voice got loud too. I cut the television up, not wanting to hear what they said, but couldn't block it all out.

"Where have you been, damnit?" she said.

He wouldn't answer directly. "Leave me the hell alone," he kept saying. I wished she would.

Finally I jumped up, cut the movie off, and was about to go out the door. I couldn't take any of it much longer without starting to cry, and then here he comes busting out of the bedroom, saying, "Go to hell!"

Then there's that moment. Daddy's in the living room and Mama's standing in the hallway. I look first at one, then the other. They look at me. Daddy's red in the face. Mad. Mama has that pleading look in *her* eyes now. I see how much she hurts, how she can't stand it. Then she's got tears in her eyes. They are the last thing I see. I walk out. God help me.

I drove for an hour or more, first around the Loop Road, and then later toward Demarville. On the other side of the Loop, I saw Daddy fly by. I knew he'd been headed out of the house, just like me, knew Mama would be left alone, like always. I didn't know where Daddy was headed. At least that's what I told myself.

After coming back from Demarville, I turned off toward The Landing. I drove down to the campsites and found Jimmy Neal sitting on top of the picnic table, beating a stick against the ground. The dust cloud settled slow behind my car. I got out and went and sat beside him. He didn't even look up. The river was still as could be. No wind blew ripples on it. No barge passed.

"I've missed you," he said.

Even though I suddenly missed him, I still didn't say anything. He finally looked at me, then put his arm around me, hugged me tight, kissed me on the neck. He was so gentle, but I felt like there was nothing he could do, that there was no way for him to hold me that would make me feel better, so I did a stupid thing, the only thing it seems I know how to do. I pushed him away. I thought of Mama then, how I do her that way too, how she probably needed me right then and I'd run off, just like Daddy. She's alone, I thought. Hurting and crying.

"What's been wrong?" he said then. "Has something happened? Did I do something?"

All I could say to that was, "Where's your daddy?" acting like he hadn't said a word.

"Daddy got cleaned up, left in the truck awhile ago."

He'd gone to see that woman. Louise Potter's her name. I don't even like to say it. She does hair over in Demarville, and everytime you see her, she's wearing her own a different way. Usually something wild. And she ain't a real blonde.

"I wish you'd tell me what's wrong," he said again.

I tried to this time, but there was a hard thing in my throat and I couldn't get a word up past it. My throat just closed around it.

"Tell me, damnit," he said. He looked at me, reached his hand out, and touched my arm. I jerked away.

"I don't like being ignored like I have been," he said. There was a hard tone in his voice. He'd had about as much as he would take, and it surprised me, like when he said he wouldn't go to the river.

His daddy pulled up then, got out of the truck. His hair was all messed up and a ripped sleeve hung from his left arm. Dried blood was crusted over one eye, and blood stained his shirt too. He looked at us both, started to smile but didn't.

"One of the hazards. Usually it's a husband," he said, "but this time . . ." He stopped, caught himself, looked directly at me, then at the ground. His lip was swollen and purple.

"The hell with both of you," Jimmy Neal said and walked off through the woods.

His daddy started to say something to me, but didn't. He just walked on in the trailer, left me standing there, alone. Now that I think about what happened, what I found out at home, I guess there was nothing he could have said to me that would've mattered.

"I know," I heard Mama yell when I got back to the house. Daddy's truck was parked in the drive and the front door stood wide open. I walked in, took one look at Daddy, and saw the blood on his shirt, the welt on his face, and knew then, knew what Mama knew and had known—Louise Potter. Jimmy Neal must have known too. How could he not when his daddy was involved?

Mama started to say something else, but looked at me and shook her head, then walked into their bedroom and slammed the door so hard it felt like the whole house had the shakes.

"Looks like your Mama and me ain't going to be staying together," he said. The blood on him wasn't his, but he looked mortally wounded the way it was smeared across his stomach. Looked like something had broken him open.

He walked on outside then, got in his truck. He cranked it, slipped it into gear, and backed out. He was gone.

I started toward Mama's door and called out to her. She didn't answer. I called again and tried the doorknob, but it was locked. I stood there afraid, aching inside, like someone might feel if they'd just had convulsions. "Mama," I said.

"Go away. Leave me alone," she finally said. And then I heard, without her actually saying it, "What about before? What about all those other times? Where were you then?"

I went to my room, climbed into bed without bothering to change, and waited for sleep.

The morning was hot. I looked out the kitchen window and saw Mama in the garden. She held the hoe like a weapon and ripped the ground open with it. She didn't look like my mother at all, not anybody's mother. I put shoes on and went out to her. "What's going to happen, Mama?"

"I don't know," she said. "I'm sorry I spoke to you like I did last night. I was upset." It was an apology, but didn't sound like one somehow. She kept working with the hoe, looking like some woman who'd worked in the field all her life, one of those women who are strong as some men. It may sound strange, but I was a little afraid of her.

"So where did Daddy go?" I said.

She didn't answer.

"Will he be back?"

"I think so," she said.

"Will he *stay* when he comes back?"

"Don't know," she said.

"Do you want him to stay?"

"I don't know."

That night Daddy called and told Mama he was at the hotel in Demarville. She said she didn't know when he was coming home and wouldn't tell me anything else he said, even when I asked.

I went back down to Jimmy Neal's late, after I thought his daddy would be gone. I didn't know if he was still seeing that woman, but I knew he'd be somewhere. I felt real bad and still didn't know what I wanted from Jimmy Neal—just something I felt like I'd never had, I guess.

A light burned inside the trailer and the little window air conditioner rattled. He was in there. I knocked and he opened the door. "Hey," he said, but not much else. He opened the door on up wide, and I climbed up the steps and went inside. He sat in a chair, and I sat over on a small sofa that had a tear in one cushion. I'd never been in the trailer before. It smelled of the river, but after a while I didn't notice it anymore. The place wasn't as messy as you think it might have been, there was just that smell at first, the Tennahpush.

We sat and looked at each other for a while. We were both nervous.

"Why'd you come back?" he said.

Told him I didn't know. "You don't want me here?" I said.

"I didn't say that," he said.

"You're acting like you don't."

He didn't say anything to that, just looked at me with those blue eyes. I didn't know what he could be thinking about me. Didn't know if he wanted me there or not. I hoped he did. I told him about Daddy then and what happened at the house. He already knew part of it.

He seemed a long way off from me. I wanted him close, but the more I talked about Daddy, the farther away he felt, the farther away everything felt. It was like our fathers were in our way—what they'd done. I got out of the chair and walked over to him and reached down and took his hands in mine. They were rough from work, a little dirty. He looked at me with those water-color eyes of his, and I pulled him up out of the chair and led him over to the torn sofa. We sat down next to each other and then I kissed him. I could smell his dried sweat. It was strong and sharp. I was nearest the light switch so I got up and cut it off. When I came back I unbuttoned his shirt real slow and ran my hands over his chest and shoulders and finally kissed his stomach. He took a deep breath and his chest swelled, and then he slowly let the air out like he was having trouble breathing. I knew what I was doing was making him breathe like that, and I knew suddenly I could do anything I wanted with him.

I took his hands, put them on my stomach, and pushed them up to my breasts. He waited, but finally let his fingers close around them. He was gentle. I kissed him then, pulled away and unbuttoned my top, and took his hands again and made him pull the top open and off my shoulders. It fell. I knew not to wait on him, so I unhooked my bra in front and in the dim light of the trailer could see the look on his face, like he didn't believe what was in front of him. His eyes were so wide. I put my open hand at the back of his head and pulled him toward me. It didn't take much. His mouth found me. It was wet and warm, but it wasn't enough. I wasn't going to be satisfied with just that because I'd had that before, and because I was determined to have more it was almost like I couldn't enjoy what I was having him do to me because I had to keep thinking what to do next. Then I felt like I was the guy, knowing all of a sudden what goes through a guy's mind when he's with a girl trying to get her to do what he wants. I kissed him again and at the same time reached down and unbuttoned his blue jeans, which was easy because I'd done that before. I had done the thing that I was fixing to do with other boys, but I knew this time that this wasn't going to be all either. In some ways I was scared and in some ways not because I had decided, Okay, this is it. It will happen now. I'll make him do it. It was something I wanted, needed.

So I did the thing I'd done before, but stopped when I knew I had better stop. He made little noises way down inside, and he was still breathing in the way I was making him breathe and as long as he was doing that I had him. But at the same time I felt sick with myself because I did know what I was doing, mostly, did know that I had him. I unbuttoned my jeans and slipped them off as fast and as easy as possible. Then slipped off, with one hand mostly, the last little thing that needed slipping off, and there I was, naked, straddled across his lap with him sitting on top of the torn place. It was like I could see myself there, like standing off, looking at the both of us. Then I was scared for one second, and felt cold with the air conditioner blowing right on me, so cold, but so determined, too, that I couldn't think about being scared. Then I shut my eyes against that cold air blowing into my face, shut myself off from everything, and lowered myself onto him.

It hurt, burned almost. All I could think then was, Why does it have to hurt? I could feel him moving. And I thought too, How can it burn when I feel so cold? I had my arms behind his back and wanted to hold him, liked his holding me, the way his arms were tight around my back, but it still hurt and I thought, Does it always hurt? Does everything have to hurt? Is this the way it is?

He stopped then and pressed his face against my breasts and let out a long breath. I could feel it on my skin.

I pulled away from him and crawled to the end of the sofa and sat there in a tight bundle, so cold. I pulled my top over me then. He held his hand out to me, but I didn't take it. He moved closer. I wanted him to get up and put his clothes on, but he didn't. He sat there right next to me with nothing on, not moving at all. I still hurt. He looked at me, put his hand on my bent knee. "Do you still love me?" he said.

I sat there all cold and tight and hurting. "No," I said. I didn't know another word to say, seemed like.

He left town right away, sooner than he had to. He rode by the house once, but he didn't stop. His daddy and the rest of the crew are still here. I'll be glad when they're gone. I want them out of here. I hate the sight of their trucks.

But even after they're gone, I know I'll still think of Jimmy Neal. I keep thinking now about what he said to me, him wanting to know if I *still* loved him, like maybe I really *did* love him, or could love him. And there was me thinking how smart I was all along, but he knew more than me. If I loved him, maybe I can be loved. Maybe he loved me. I know he never meant to hurt me, would have died if he'd known he had. And so why did I hurt him? How can we deep down come to want something so nice and right and pure, and make it all so ugly and mean?

I think about how I saw Jimmy Neal that first day and picked him, just like that, like he was something to be taken off a shelf and played with. It makes me sick with myself. Mama says that you can't just take someone, they have to give themselves, and that maybe some people can do that and others can't. I'm scared to death I'm one that can't. It seems strange to be scared of something you can't do, but maybe that's the worst thing of all, the thing to fear most.

Daddy's back home now. I don't know what's going to happen. He still stays gone a lot, but not as much. He isn't seeing that woman, I don't think. He still walks right past me when he comes through a room, but the other night he knocked on my door late, stuck his head in, and just said, "Good night," real quiet. I asked Mama if Daddy'll ever be able to give himself like we'd talked about. "Never as much as we'll want," she said. Then she cried a little. I held her tight.

Fires

IT BURNED QUICK. We stood way back, all the way over to Miss Sanders' trailer, watching them big sheets of aluminum fall to the ground, all black and scorched looking, like the bottom of a old pan. I knew it was going to catch up fast, especially with the coal oil poured all over the chairs and the rugs and everything else. I even had a little on my clothes and was scared Grandmama was going to smell it on me. I kept wanting to move away from her, but she held me tight and said everything was going to be all right, not to worry. It wasn't like it was my fault. I felt a hurt when she said that.

The heat was so bad we couldn't get no closer. Fire kept leaping up high from the inside, and the smoke was black looking, like some big ugly cloud. I could see in my mind all the beds and the chairs and them thin wood walls burning. And the television. Then I thought all about Grandmama's things again, the things she loved—the box with all the old pictures in it of Granddaddy, who I never did know, and her old sewing machine what she was so proud of, and the silver comb Granddaddy give her on their wedding day. I started crying then, thinking about what all Grandmama lost. It hurt me like they was my things. But she herself wasn't crying. She just looked at that trailer like it was nothing but a big old pile of brush burning or some leaves or something.

"It be all right, child," Grandmama said again, then put her big arms tighter around me. I could see the white flour spotted on them, smell it too—got a clean and light kind of smell to it —and I knew she'd been making a cake with Miss Sanders. A cake for me maybe. "Don't be crying. Everything be all right," she said.

Then Uncle Henry said, "Yes child, don't you worry none. We find another place to live."

He said *we*. Like it him take care of us. But he don't do nothing.

Grandmama'd been over to Miss Sanders' most all of the afternoon, and she had told me I could play outside close by. Uncle Henry, that's Grandmama's brother, he was supposed to be watching me, but he was laying his old lazy self down by the creek, like always, taking himself a drink. I know cause I slipped down there and spied him. But when I hollered, he got there first cause I called him instead of yelling "Fire." I didn't want people coming too fast. By the time Grandmama come running along with the others, it too late. There ain't no fire department to call. Couldn't nothing be saved. I'd done what I had to.

That trailer went on and fell in on itself, and the fire started to die on down cause there wasn't nothing left for to burn. Then I saw one thing that didn't burn sticking up out of everything else, Grandmama's sewing machine. It was all scorched and black, but it was still there, and I thought about how if somebody tried to use it they'd burn their hands down to the bone.

"They sure burns up quick," Uncle Henry said. That what he always saying. Some cloud would come up and then storm, and Grandmama'd say, like some folks make a joke, "A trailer'll draw a tornado." But it ain't no joke with her. Then Uncle Henry'd say she was right and that he didn't like living in no trailer no how. He was all the time saying he was going to move on. And I'd want to say, "So go on then." But he'd just sit there and say, "And when they burns up, they burns up fast, and you best hope you ain't asleep." That was what he'd say. Every time. *They burns up quick.* I remembered that.

I'd been living with Grandmama for a year almost. I moved in right after my daddy was killed in a car wreck. Mama was still down on the river. The Tennahpush. But she said I had to stay with Grandmama awhile. She said it was best. Grandmama told me how it all was. She told me how that night job at the jug factory Mama had got was all she could find. I sure couldn't stay by myself at night, and Mama had to sleep in the day. And too, she said Mama wasn't herself exactly since Daddy been killed. Mama had to get herself right so she could have me back again. She said Mama was a young mama and maybe sometimes a young mama, especially one what done lost a husband, can't handle things too good. "How young is my mama?" I asked her. "She young yet, child. She had you when she wasn't but fourteen," she said. "Was my daddy a young daddy?" I asked her then. "Yes, he was, child," she said. "And he turned out to be a good man and a good daddy. Hard working."

I missed my daddy. Sometimes I'd think about that wreck and picture him in the car when it got hit, see his head hitting the window, see his blood like I was there. I tried not to think about it, but I did.

That day of the fire I was all set to move back down with Mama, like I'd planned on. I hoped Grandmama would come too, but Uncle Henry would have to go live somewhere else because there wouldn't be enough room for *him*. It too small a house for him to be there with us. Then everything would be all right, and Uncle Henry wouldn't be able to do all his things anymore. He'd be gone.

But before the ashes of the trailer was even cold Miss Sanders said, "Y'all going to move in with me." Told us, didn't ask. Right quick I said, "There ain't enough room for all us in your trailer. We won't fit. I know we won't." I thought, This ain't how it supposed to be at all. This ain't the way. This ain't going to do no good. Then I looked over at Uncle Henry and he just started nodding his head, like he was all ready to move in.

"They two more bedrooms, and child, you can sleep on the sofa," Miss Sanders said. "It fold out. Make a nice bed. You won't have your own private room, though, like you been having."

Then I thought, Well maybe this will work all right. Not having my own room. And Miss Sanders do got the nicest trailer. Been here a long time, ever since the river flooded so bad and the county brought in these trailers for black folks what got flooded out.

So we all moved on in with Miss Sanders and it looked like

things was going to be all right, what with me sleeping on the sofa in the living room. Miss Sanders was right. It did make a nice bed. Real comfortable. Only thing was, seemed like Grandmama knew there was still something on my mind. Bad on my mind. She kept watching me, asking me, "What wrong child?"

One day she and Miss Sanders was sitting out on the stoop, snapping beans. I walked by and Grandmama grab hold of me. "Now tell me what wrong," she said. She wasn't going to let me by with saying "nothing." Not this time. So I said how bad I felt about what she done lost in the fire, her home and all the little things she loved, which was the truth. I couldn't get it out of my head. "But child," she said, "I didn't do nothing but rent that trailer. I didn't own it. And all them things like that old sewing machine and silver comb, they just things. I just glad you be all right. I would of let myself get burned up to save you." I listened to what all she said, but I started crying. She told me again how it wasn't like it was my fault that everything burned, and then I really busted loose.

After that when Grandmama saw me looking sad and what all, she knew what the cause of it was. Or thought she did. Just like when I came to live with her and Uncle Henry after Daddy got killed. She knew my daddy being gone was what was making me sad and quiet all the time. And it was, but after a while there was that something else too—Uncle Henry. Only I didn't tell Grandmama about that. I couldn't. Not then and not now. I couldn't even tell Mama. And if my daddy had been still alive, I couldn't of told him most of all. He always told me what a good little girl I was, that I was his baby, but I didn't feel like I was good no more. I wanted to keep being good for him, that way if I kept doing something for him, it wouldn't seem like he was gone. It would be like the wreck never happened.

So I slept on the sofa in the living room every night, and it looked like things was working *kind of* like I hoped they would. I knew Miss Sanders was in the front bedroom right through the door that I could see when I laid there with the covers up around my neck. They was just enough light that came through the window to shine a little on her doorknob, and I'd look at that piece of brass light till I went off to sleep, knowing I could get up and run knock, say I was feeling sick or whatever if I had to. And I knew Grandmama was at the other end of the trailer. Only if she hadn't snored so loud. Everybody knew when she was asleep and when not. Everybody.

The problem got to be that the bathroom was in the hall. I can't make it through most nights without having to pee, so I'd get up and step down to the bathroom, trying hard to be quiet. One night Uncle Henry, he heard me and came out his door when I was passing. He heard Grandmama snoring too, so he knew she was asleep, and knew Miss Sanders' door always closed. It done started again, I thought. And it did. It started back bad.

So it didn't work. Then I thought, Well, what am I going to do now? If I try to hold my pee, I might pee in the bed and ruin Miss Sanders' nice sofa. So I thought on it.

I tried taking myself outdoors and squatting behind the trailer where it was good and dark. I'd be scared of the dark but more scared of him. I'd make myself breathe real slow, make the scared go away, then pull down my pajamas and go long enough where I wouldn't have to go again. Then one night up he came out of the dark and that was the end of me going outside. He was mad. Real mad.

Every night got to be some kind of rough. I'd be laying in bed trying to hold myself, trying not to pee. I'd put a pillow down there and squeeze it tight with my legs. Wouldn't drink no water before bed. Sometimes that worked. I wouldn't have to go. I'd be safe. Uncle Henry wouldn't risk coming into where I was at with Miss Sanders' door so close. But it didn't usually work. Not drinking water that is. I'd still wake up, but it would be just later on in the night, and I'd think, Maybe this night he be asleep and won't hear. Or maybe this be one of his off nights. I never knew when he'd be there and when he wouldn't.

Then the worst thing what could happen did. Miss Sanders said one night sitting in front of the television that one reason she wanted us to move on in was because she'd done started thinking since she getting so old, she *might* just move on down to the other side of Demarville and live with her sister. She said we could stay right on and rent her trailer. I thought, Now everything be as bad as before. Ain't nothing have changed. Grandmama said, "What's wrong child? You ain't got to look so sad. You see Miss Sanders again. She ain't going to be that far." When Grandmama said that, I knew there wasn't no *might* to it.

That night while I looked at the little old piece of light on Miss Sanders' doorknob, watched it kind of glowing-like, I kept wondering about how long it was going to be before she was going to move, about how much time I had. Then I thought, *They burns quick.* But I didn't want to be thinking that. Tried to put it out of my mind. I turned one way, then another, and thought for a while about my mama, how she'd put my hair in cornrows. Then I thought about my daddy. Saw him in that wreck. Saw blood on his head. I got to be good for him, I thought. I got to. He said I was his good little girl. Finally I went on to sleep. When I woke up I had to walk down the hall and pee, and Uncle Henry got me, just like he did the two nights after. All of three nights in a row. Worst ever.

After that I started thinking, This can't keep on. It just can't. Then one night Uncle Henry said, "When Miss Sanders gone, you have you a room again and it be like it was after you came up from down on the river." He said that and kind of smiled at me, like I liked what he did. I turned away and wouldn't look at him there in the dark. But I could still smell his old sweaty self. His hair always smelled like he washed it in mop water.

One day when Grandmama was busy inside the trailer and Uncle Henry slipped off down to the creek, I started to walking. I had a stick with me and punched it along the ground. I figured if a snake came along, I could hit him with it. I knew the way I was going, and knew it was going to be a long walk, but I didn't care. I didn't even let myself think about how worried Grandmama was going to be.

By the time I got to the road that goes down to the river, I was all sweaty and tired as could be, but I kept on. I was thinking about Mama, and Daddy, too. It was almost like they was both going to be home when I got there, waiting on me. Daddy would pick me up, spin me around, like he always did.

After I walked about another mile, a big lady in a car stopped beside me. It the first car I'd seen in a long while. "Ain't you Cookie's child?" she said. I told her I was. "Lord, child. What you doing out by yourself?"

"I'm going to see my mama," I said, and when I said the

word "mama," I about started to cry, but I didn't let myself.

"Well, come on and get in. I'll take you to your mama."

So she drove me to the house and knocked on the door. I was so glad to be home. In a little bit Mama opened the door and her eyes was all sleepy looking, but they got big when she saw me.

She thanked the lady that brung me, then took me inside and told me I shouldn't of tried to walk by myself. "What would your daddy think?" she said. "What?" She said she should whip me. I didn't say nothing, just stood there.

She called Grandmama and told her she'd bring me back directly, then fixed me a big glass of tea in the kitchen. We sat down in the front room on the sofa.

"I want to stay here with you," I said. "I want to sleep in my old room."

"I'd like that, too, but your mama got to work tonight. You know that."

"I don't mean just tonight. I mean every night," I said.

She looked away then and didn't say nothing for a long while. I sat there with my tea in my hand and started thinking about my daddy. I felt almost like he might come walking in the room, and say, "Of course my baby can stay," but I knew he wouldn't cause all of a sudden I seen him in that wreck again, seen the blood on him.

"Not yet," Mama said. "I know you don't understand, but the time ain't right just yet."

"But I want to come home," I said. "I can't live up there no more."

"Why can't you live there?"

I didn't say nothing.

"Y'all in a nice place, and your Grandmama gon' fix it all up, make it feel like home. Put some pictures on the wall. You'll see."

I put my glass down and climbed up in her lap. She held me and rocked me back and forth, even though I was too big. I smelled of her. She always wear a nice lady's scent, sweet-like. I wanted to ask her again to let me come live at home, but I didn't. Seemed like more and more I couldn't say what I wanted to say or tell what I wanted to tell, so I just sat there and thought about Daddy. "You a good little girl," I could hear him saying.

After a while Mama said she had to take me on back. I just hung on tight. Finally she got me up, though, and she went back into her room. Then I saw her slip into the bathroom and close the door. She ran the water in the sink for a long, long time before she came out. I kept saying, "What you doing, Mama?" through the door, but she wouldn't say nothing.

When we got back to Grandmama's, Mama came in and sat and visited. She told Grandmama not to whip me for going off. Not this time. "But don't do that again," she said to me. "It dangerous." I promised her I wouldn't.

It started to get dark, and Mama got up and hugged me and walked out the door. I followed her part way to the car and then stopped and watched while she got in. "I miss you, Mama," I said. But she had done slammed the door and didn't hear. Then seemed like she drove off quick, like she couldn't even make herself look back at me. When I turned around, Grandmama was standing on the stoop looking down on me. She looked right sad, like she'd just found out somebody died. She took me in her arms. Uncle Henry was standing there behind her looking at me. He looked sad, too, but that night he came on in my room.

❦

Grandmama went to Demarville the next day, early. She said she might go see Miss Sanders, and she told Uncle Henry to watch me. I knew how he'd watch me. He'd go down to the creek and have himself a drink, like always. He never came after me in the day. He didn't pay no mind.

Soon as Grandmama left, there went Uncle Henry. I knew this had to be the time, and my heart started beating like before, and in my mind I still heard them words Uncle Henry'd always said. So while them words is ringing, I run to the cabinet where the garbage can is at, where Grandmama had always kept the little lamp and the jug in our old trailer for when the lights went out. And I see she done been up to Anderson's store since the fire and the move and got it. It sitting there just like I pictured it. Coal oil got a strong smell to it. Ain't bad as gasoline, but it bad enough. When it soak into bed sheets and a chair cushion and the curtains at a window, it ain't no undoing it. I do like before. Go to Uncle Henry's room first and pour some of it all round and wish that's all I have to burn— his room with maybe him in it—and then it all go away, like nothing never happened, like he never was here and it just be me and Grandmama and Mama. And Daddy, too. But it did happen, and he is here, I think, and this the only way I know to get rid of him. It bound to work this time, I tell myself. It got to. It will.

Then I run to Grandmama's room with my heart beating like it going to bust, and I can't hardly breathe right my breath be coming so fast. I hate what I'm doing but I pour it all over her room, then run to my room, what was Miss Sanders', and pour the rest. I take me some matches from the same cabinet and go back to Grandmama's room. I strike one against the side of the box, smell that little sharp match-burning kind of smell like when you ain't going to do nothing but burn some trash or something. Only I know this ain't trash. I put the flame to the sheets, then run do it in Uncle Henry's room, then to my room cause it closest to the door. I run out but I don't holler "Fire! Fire!" I call "Uncle Henry! Uncle Henry!" just like before, cause I want anybody that might hear to hear me calling after *somebody.*

By the time Grandmama came pulling up fast in the car, with Miss Sanders sitting next to her, it was about burned down. Somebody had done called them, and they came on in a hurry, but it wasn't nothing they could do. This time Grandmama just kept walking back and forth saying how she couldn't believe it done happened again. How could it? I didn't say nothing.

"Where was you at child when it started?" she said.

"I was playing outside," I told her, hating how I got to lie and scared she going to know the truth somehow.

"Least you wasn't in there," she said. "Thank goodness for that." Then she looked at Uncle Henry. "Where was you at?" she said.

He didn't say nothing right away. Just looked at the ground.

"He was down on the creek," I said.

"But I kept checking back on her," he said real quick. "She was playing right outside the trailer the whole time." I was real glad he said that last part.

"You supposed to be watching this child all the time," she said. She was mad. I could tell. She kept staring hard at him. "What if she'd been in there and didn't know the trailer was on fire until it was too late? What then? You wouldn't of been no help."

"But she all right," he say, looking at me mean, like he knew something maybe.

Grandmama didn't say nothing else, just kept staring, and he turned on around and headed off back down to the creek. Grandmama went to walking, like before. "How could it happen again?" she said.

"It don't matter how," Miss Sanders said. "It just the way it be. It God's will. And you be glad this child all right. And Henry all right."

Grandmama made a kind of snorting sound through her nose when she said Uncle Henry's name.

Mama came pulling up in a little while. She got out the car and came and picked me up. "Is my baby all right?" she said. I'm too heavy for her, but she didn't put me down. It got to work this time, I think. Ain't nowhere else to go now.

For weeks all people could talk about was how both them trailers could burn up like that. I was scared. They kept saying what bad luck it was. Hard luck. Said it wasn't like Grandmama deserved nothing terrible like that, not like some folks does maybe. Seemed like people looked at me funny. One day Grandmama come up to me and sat me down in her big lap. "If anybody be saying mean things to you, child, about them fires, you come tell your grandmama. You hear? I ain't gon' have no one talking ugly to you, telling lies about you. You a sweet child."

I was even more scared then. But I didn't tell. I couldn't. Not no one. If I did, it would be like Daddy would know then, know everything. And I had to keep being good for him.

Fires

Me and Grandmama done moved in with Mama, and it look like we going to stay. Uncle Henry living down in Dawes Quarter now and that where he belongs at. Down there with them sorry folks. He can stay there. Mama says sometimes when bad happens, it make good things happen. She says I'm her daughter and ain't nobody else supposed to take care of me anyway. She says she forgot that for a little while. Says she want me to forgive her.

So now Mama puts me to bed every night and wake me up every morning. She braid my hair like she used to and bring me home a little candy like I like sometimes. That make me feel good. I love my mama, and I know she love me. But I don't feel good all the way yet. I ain't got to see Uncle Henry, but I keep thinking about him and what all he done. I'm going to forget all about it, though, let it burn away. That's what I waiting on. Want it to burn out of my mind. Sometimes I see that picture I get of my daddy with blood on his head, and it seem like that picture don't go away—and it been over a year now. So I worried that some things maybe don't never go away. They stay in your mind. Some things maybe you just can't burn. They scorch and turn black, but don't burn. Ever.

The Cemetery

SHE WAS TAKING a walk, alone, and had worked her way up a knoll through the scattered pines and cedars and the bare hardwoods that rose toward the November sky, when she came upon the faded marble and granite stones. They looked like gray and white ghosts, she thought, rising suddenly from the cold ground, nearly hidden there among the thick, dark trunks of the trees. She felt oddly as though she had made some sort of discovery, a discovery of things that had lain awkwardly in silence and in time. It occurred to her that the dead—for each day now—meant more to her than the living.

In September, two months before she discovered the stones of the old Caulfield-Hitt cemetery, Lydia Sayre had lain in her own cool sweat at the hospital in Demarville, delivering her first-born. When the small body had finally slid down, she'd waited to receive it, to hold it, but she had caught only a glimpse of the gray, wet child as the doctor gripped it and turned away.

"Boy or girl?" she'd gasped.

The nurse, a small, dark-complexioned woman, looked at her and answered quietly, "A girl." The nurse's face was drawn taut, and the lines across her brow were pulled into tight arches. Her eyes were dark.

"Is she all right?" Lydia asked.

"We're going to do all we can," the nurse answered.

Later, as she lay in a private room, Robert, still in his work clothes, his hair wet with sweat, hurried to her.

"We've got a little girl," he had cried, almost like a child, as he leaned over the rail of the hospital bed, clutching the metal. "Our little girl. Can you believe it?"

Exhausted, she could only gaze at him.

Two days later the child was dead. Three days later it was given its name, Susan Amelia, and then it was buried.

Her first weeks after the death were passed in a kind of numb sorrow, one that seemed to start from some deep and hidden place within her and to spread outward, causing a dull ache even all the way into her wrists and ankles. After a month, and then another, the ache began to give way to a silent, direction-less anger. But the anger, when it rose, at least gave her the strength to move. She began to take long walks, sometimes into Riverfield up the narrow asphalt road that she had known all her life, sometimes into the woods behind the house that she and Robert had lived in two years before she found the cemetery.

After looking in surprise at the stones, and wondering vague-ly why she had never known they were there, she was now even more startled by the hunter, dressed in dirt-smeared, camou-flaged coveralls and sitting motionless against one of the granite blocks. He peered into the dense trees below. He had not seen her, she thought, and he looked as if he were a stone himself, a sculpted sentinel guarding the dead. She remained quiet, watching him until distant noises—voices of men and the deep baying of hounds—filtered through the trees; then she turned and walked quietly back through the woods to the empty house.

Robert came home late from the paper mill. After he walked into the house and lay down on the flower-print sofa in the den for a few minutes, she put food out on the table and called him, then sat across from him while he ate. She watched as he unbuttoned his workshirt, and she noticed that the lettering across the front—Gulf States Paper Mill—was beginning to fade. He had been in the habit of asking what she'd done while he was at work, but her answers—"just thinking" and "nothing"—over the last two months had made him pause and gaze curiously at her. Finally he'd stopped asking. There had been the solid touch of his hand during the funeral, his flesh hard against her, but after that, nothing seemed gentle, living, warm.

After she'd sat for a time staring at the hands in her lap, looking at the blue veins running across her bones, she finally spoke.

"You need a new shirt," she said. Somehow the statement seemed ridiculous.

"Yes," he said, fixing his eyes on her. "Did you walk today?"

"Yes."

She didn't want to say more, and she hoped that he would leave it at that.

"Where?" he asked.

"Just out," she said. As soon as she'd said it, she realized her tone was wrong.

"Just out?" he half mimicked. "Out where? You think you might could tell me?"

"I went for a walk behind the house."

She rose quietly from the chair and collected all of the dishes she could carry, then went to the kitchen. She stayed there, washing the dishes with a great and purposeful clatter, banging them vigorously against the sides of the sink, even after Robert had finished eating and had gone to the bedroom. She sat then and watched the small clock that was part of the stove. When the bedroom lights had been out for fifteen minutes, she went quietly to the bed. She lay awake beside him, watching him, listening to him breathe.

The graveyard was unguarded when she returned the following afternoon. It seemed at first unnatural to her that the hunter wasn't there, that no one watched over the stones, as though some law were being broken. She began to walk among the graves, counting; there were more than twenty. She kept losing count because of the way the markers were scattered among the old trunks, but it seemed somehow important that she know exactly how many there were. She started over, but she saw then that the graves surrounded her in a rough circle with no clear beginning or end. She stopped in front of one of the stones which had been pushed up and tilted by the roots of a huge oak; for a moment she imagined great hands beneath it, pushing the stone slowly from the ground, and she wondered if the remains of the bodies had been disturbed in the same way.

She looked again at the other graves. Many were bound on each end by a headstone and a small, square foot marker. She studied the graves more closely and discovered that many of them were small: the graves of children. Some had died at two or three years of age, others had lived only a few months; some had lived only days. The earliest was that of a boy named David Caulfield—Born September 23, 1821, Died December 26, 1821, *Son of John D. and Mary J. / Taken Back Unto God*. She stood back and stared at the almost illegible engraving. She envisioned an empty corridor and saw the corridor's floor littered with the same dead gold, orange, red, and brown leaves that lay scattered over the boy's sunken grave. There were rich colors in death, she thought.

She moved from stone to stone and saw repeated the names Caulfield and Hitt. Many of the graves were sunken, and she found herself wondering if the souls of the people left their bodies only when they were buried, causing the earth to slowly hollow out and sink with time. She thought that perhaps a burial was not complete until the grave had sunk.

One stone was wedged so tightly between two sweet gum trees that the bark of each of them had grown in around the edges of it, holding it like two great wooden hands. The marker was of light gray, the name *Margaret Caulfield Hitt* engraved across the top and beneath it the dates July 11, 1898, and October 14, 1919, *And Daughter*.

She stood for a moment before the stone, puzzling, then sat down among the leaves beside it and read the small, stylized carving at the bottom, *Bringing Life, Life Was Taken / A Child And Mother Gone To God*.

She leaned across the sunken grave and ran her hand softly over the stone. It felt rough and cold. She traced the words at the bottom, running her fingertips into the skilled, graceful lettering, staining her fingers with the dirt of years. She read the dates again, and she realized that the girl had died at twenty-one. She tried then to imagine the young mother, and in her mind an image formed of a small dark girl with long black hair and brooding eyes. The girl was standing, and Lydia saw in her arms what looked to be a child wrapped in a blanket, but she couldn't see the child or hear it; it lay completely still. Slowly the girl bent forward, her long hair falling loosely in front of her. For a moment Lydia thought she could see the top of the baby's head, but the blanket still shrouded the child.

The image snapped away.

There were several Caulfields in Demarville, she thought as she walked away from the stone. They owned businesses in the town and were prominent people. But Lydia didn't know any of them; she only recognized the name, mentioned now and then over the years.

Robert came home late in the afternoon. His shift had been changed and he got home earlier now. He came into the house, soiled and silent. She began to prepare supper while he bathed, trying to concentrate on the meal, but as she worked at the counter, the image of the girl and the covered child came suddenly to her, moved without her permission into her mind.

Robert came from the bedroom. He was clean-shaven and dressed in a clean shirt and pants. He walked into the kitchen and stood near her, watching her work, not speaking. He was so close that she could smell the soap on his body, and she felt as if he were trying to look inside her, to know what she was thinking, to know then what to say. He lifted a platter and carried it to the table.

"You been out today? Been nice out," he said when he came back.

"I just walked up the road a short ways," she said after a moment.

She put the rest of the food on the table, and they sat across from one another. The hot smell of the meal filled the room; it rose from the table and drifted in from the kitchen. Robert began to talk about work. She listened vaguely and nodded to the breaks in the rhythm of his voice.

"Do you know any of the Caulfields?" she asked suddenly during a lull in his speech.

He paused with his fork halfway up from his plate and looked at her. He smiled and seemed to be glad that she was finally interested in something.

"Don't really know any of them too good," he said. "Know them when I see them on the street. One owns the lumberyard. They've all got money, especially Miss Mamie. She's a spinster, old as the hills. She don't get out anymore."

He took another bite of the food. She wanted to press him further, but she held herself back, not wanting to have to explain why she was interested in the Caulfields.

"Used to live over here a long time ago," he finally continued. "Them two big old chimneys that stand out in the woods right back off the road, they was part of their house."

"That's right." She remembered now. "Some of the old people used to call that the Caulfield Place."

"They left when it burned."

"When was that?" she said carefully.

"I don't know. Long time ago. It must've been a fine house, judging from the size of them chimneys."

Later, in the living room, she sat with a book in her lap, staring at the print, but no matter how hard she tried to concentrate on the words, she found that she could think only about the girl. Robert came into the room quietly and sat down, his shadow moving across the wall in the light from the floor lamp.

"You ever see the old graveyard when you were out walking?" he asked. "That why you've had the Caulfields on your mind?"

"I've seen it out there," she said.

"Wish you'd told me. It's better for you not to be going out there any more. It ain't good for you."

"How do you know what's *good* for me?" she heard herself snap.

"Well, it's damned sure the dead don't need you out there."

She went back the next day. The sun shone hard and bright through the trees and reflected dully from the gray and white stones. She sat down beside Margaret Hitt's grave and read once more the words carved into the marker; then she stared blankly toward the sky that was streaked now with thin clouds. The image came suddenly—strong and sharp. The girl stood dressed in a housecoat, solid black with large black buttons. Her long dark hair was nearly the same color as the coat and looked almost like a hood. Her eyes, although dark, seemed to illuminate the image, to give it a center. In her arms she held a blanket that covered the child completely, and the heavy, coarse, woolen material was soiled and worn; the child lay motionless under it. Lydia wondered then why the girl's eyes and not the child were the center of the image.

The sun was slightly higher now, and when she glanced toward it, the glare took the image away. She stood up and brushed leaves from the backs of her legs, then began to walk slowly among the other graves.

She tried to count the stones again, pointing her finger at each one, but she lost track after only a few yards. Giving up, she made her way through the woods to the road in front of her house and decided then to walk the short distance to the standing chimneys.

The old house had sat at the edge of the woods. Pines and oaks were growing now between the chimneys, seeming to deny the fact that there had ever been human life there. Both of the chimneys were built from large brown bricks. There were fireplaces, filled with dirt and leaves, two positioned slightly above the ground level, the others high in the air where the second story had been. In her mind she saw the walls and beams and ceilings and floors surrounding the two chimneys, and suddenly felt the lives of the Caulfields around her. She saw stiffly dressed men and women moving gracefully about on the floor above; she heard the sound of the children crying, the voices of black women coming from the kitchen, echoing through the rooms. Generations carried on their lives. They were born, grew old, and died in the rooms before her.

That afternoon, with the directory opened to the Demarville section, she found the name "Mamie E. Caulfield" near the top of a page. Not knowing what she would say, and for a moment feeling that she might be taking things too far, she slowly dialed the number.

A black woman's voice came to her through the receiver.

"Caulfield's residence," the voice said, the words ringing hard.

She hesitated. "Could I please speak with Miss Caulfield?"

"This her nap time. She can't talk now."

"Well . . . well, I just wanted to talk to her and see if I could —come visit. I live in Riverfield and I wanted to . . . I wanted to talk to her about her family."

"Oh! Yes, Miss. She love to do that. She can go on about her people. She sure can."

The house was two-story, red brick, fronted by a neatly kept lawn. An empty marble birdbath stood in the center of the wide yard.

The black woman answered the door after her third knock. The woman stood large and very dark, her hands and arms looking as if they could either break a body quickly in half or hold and shelter it as tenderly as they would a child.

"Is you the lady what called?"

Lydia nodded.

"Well, she been waiting. She love company."

Lydia followed the woman into the house.

"She want to tell you all about her people. You got to talk loud. She eighty-four and she can't hear too good."

Lydia paused in the dark and cluttered living room. Shelves of old books lined the walls, and a worn family Bible lay open on a walnut stand. It was open only to the inside of the front cover, the page filled with writing. The family's genealogy, Lydia thought, entered in by generations of women. Names and births and marriages and deaths listed with precision.

The furniture in the room, the chairs and the sofa and tables, were old, handcrafted: family heirlooms, she thought. The age and dark coloring of the wood seemed to soak up the little light that reached it. In the corner closest to the door sat a tall stack of magazines. The women on the covers were stylishly dressed, but for some other time, a time long past.

The black woman motioned Lydia out of the living room and down along a hall lined with photographs and portraits, then led her into a paneled den at the far end of the hall. Lydia's gaze fell immediately on an old woman sitting in a leather recliner. The woman's face was heavy and wrinkled, her hair tinted a pale blue color, streaks of it looking painted on with a fine brush.

"Is that you, Ethel?" the woman asked. She moved her head in a sort of circle, as if she were trying to see past something blocking her view.

"Yes, ma'am. And here's that lady, Mrs. Sayre."

The old woman's blue eyes brightened, seemed to shine through their white cloudiness.

"Oh, do come in," she said. "I was just now trying to do some recollecting."

The black woman disappeared, and Lydia slowly sat down on the red-velvet love seat that faced the recliner. The strong scent of powder, like age, came to her from the old woman.

"I have a real interest in your family," she said, forming her words slowly. "I live in Riverfield next to your family's old property and . . ."

"Yes, yes," the old woman said, cutting her off. "I was born there in 1896. In the old house. My grandfather built that house. Worked a crew of negras for a year building it. He was in the War. "

"Yes, ma'am. I see."

"What? Speak up, child."

"I said I wanted to ask you about your immediate family, your brothers and sisters."

"Why? They're all dead. I've outlived them all!" The old woman spoke as though she were proud.

"How many brothers and sisters did you have?"

"Had four brothers. They're all dead." The woman seemed irritated. "Had a sister, dead too."

"About your sister."

"Say again?"

"What was your sister's name?"

"Margaret. She died a long time ago. Can't remember exactly. It's in the book. I got a book." Then she stopped, seemed to catch her breath. "He was wounded, you know."

"Who was that?"

"Grandpa, child. Battle of Seven Pines, June of '62. He was shooting Yankees, then they shot him." The woman was silent a moment. "He was a fine man. And my papa was just like him. Everybody said so."

"How old was Margaret when she died?"

"Margaret? Died during childbirth." The woman paused, then added as though she suddenly wished to be polite, "She was a sweet girl."

"What did she look like?" Lydia asked. "Anything like you?"

"Margaret? Oh, she had light brown hair and sort of light skin. Tall, and slender. We did look something alike."

"You say she had light hair?"

"Almost blonde."

"I saw her grave in the old cemetery, that the child was buried with her."

"Yes, yes. Did that some back then. Her husband had it done like that. I got the book."

"The book?"

"Yes, child. Margaret's book. Kept up with the family in it. She wrote down everything. You come tomorrow. I'll have it out for you."

"I'd like that."

The old woman leaned toward Lydia then, as if she were ready to impart something of extreme importance. "Grandpa was buried in that old cemetery too."

Later, at home, she didn't tell Robert where she'd been, and during that night she barely spoke to him; she could think only of going back, of finding out more about Margaret Hitt. Robert seemed aware that something preoccupied her. He kept glancing at her as she sat with the newspaper in her lap. She found herself wishing that he would leave the room; it would be better to be alone than to have him watching her.

The book, a slim volume, bound in leather and filled with yellowing but intact pages, lay on a table before the divan in the living room. She was taken directly to it by the black woman who said that Miss Caulfield wasn't feeling well, and she was left alone with it there. She turned the pages carefully. Names and dates were listed for births and marriages and deaths, but there were also descriptions of family reunions and church homecomings; the people who'd attended were listed, and there were short descriptions of what some of the women wore.

The words were written in India ink. Smudges marked the pages here and there, but the lettering was neat, each letter carefully curved to completion. With the succession of each page, the writing filled more and more of each yellowed sheet. The descriptions of events and the reactions to people encountered became longer and more detailed, more personal.

As Lydia read in the dim light, she found the entry noting the writer's marriage:

On August 9, 1917, I, Margaret Caulfield, married Thomas Alvin Hitt. He is a handsome man who is fine and good. He is very strong and squarely built. He always wins at log rolling. He will make a good life for me.

As Lydia read through the description of the wedding, she thought vaguely of her own marriage and of what she had wanted from it. She remembered what she had expected from Robert, and she wondered what it was exactly that she wanted from him now. She read on.

January 28, 1918. I will have a child. Thomas has been praying for a child, he says, and we are both happy. Thomas says we need many children, and I am glad now that I am in my condition. I hope to have a boy. This is what we need.

And,

October 4, 1918. My child, David Archer Hitt, is dead. I do not know why. Women have always lost children. It is a part of our heritage and our legacy. I am not the first woman to lose a child. I have been told that I will have a large family and I know that I will. I must think only of the children to come. There will be more.

Lydia stared at the words . . . *is dead.* She studied the fine, fragile curve of the letters, noting where the flow of ink was weakest, where it barely linked all of the parts of the letters together. The words seemed almost unable to stand and to carry their meaning. Another child. So many children. A legacy. She could feel the girl's grief across the span of time, echoing within her; but she began to wonder if the girl's words were really her own, if perhaps she'd written them only to convince herself of their meaning.

My child, David Archer Hitt, is dead, she read again. Something struck her about the words as she took them in. There was something more in them, some quality, some meaning that came from the yellowed pages. *Is dead. Is dead.*

She began to move on through the book. A few events were listed: a visit by friends from the next county, mention of a special performance by the church choir, then:

> January 12, 1919. I am going to have a child. I have prayed to God for a healthy boy. This is all that I am concerned with. Thomas seems worried. A child will make him happy again. There is so much work here. Thomas won't always be able to do it by himself. He will need help.

There were a few more entries, then only empty pages filling out the book.

Lydia closed the volume and took it to the black woman and thanked her. The woman looked up solemnly from the table where she sat folding napkins. She didn't speak.

Lydia could hardly concentrate on the road home. The words that the girl had written stayed in her memory, just as they appeared on the page. When she turned off the highway onto the road to her house, the image of the girl and the child wrapped in the blanket came suddenly, left, then came again. The child lay still, covered and silent. Lydia tried to shift the image, to see the child, but she couldn't.

⁑

At four o'clock he came in. She lay on the sofa, half awake, somewhere between restless sleep and loose consciousness. She watched him walk into the kitchen, then after a little while reemerge. She'd had the lights turned off, and in the darkness of the living room he came and sat beside her, his presence somehow less real than that of the child and the girl.

"What's wrong?" he asked.

"I don't feel good."

"You sick? You need something?"

"No, it's not that," she said, looking up at him.

He turned away. "Oh."

"I have to talk to you, Robert. Will you listen?"

She could feel him physically brace himself. "Yes, go ahead," he said.

"You know I've been out in the old cemetery."

"Yes."

"There's a grave out there, the grave of a girl. She died during childbirth."

"I don't want to hear this," he said and began to push himself up. She grabbed his hands, pulled him to her.

"Please listen!"

He sat still. "All right," he said.

"I went to see Mamie Caulfield."

"You what? What's wrong with you? My God! What'd you say to her?"

"I had to see her. To find out about the girl, her sister. And I read something about the girl. She had a child who died. Just like us. It only lived a short time, and then she tried to have another, and it killed her."

"How can you have done all this?" he said, his voice rising.

"How do you think you'll get over this if you keep chasing after the dead? Leave the dead alone!"

"Robert, please. Try to understand. I've had to do this. I don't know why."

He turned from her, ran his hands across his face, and walked out, slamming the door.

She felt numb as she sat alone in the living room, her hands shaking, her thoughts confused. She remembered the pain of the delivery, and Robert's excitement, then thought of the long-dead girl and her daughter and of the graveyard's scattered stones beneath the trees.

She walked slowly up the knoll. The sun was descending and its fiery red, framed by the bare trees, colored the horizon. She reached the top of the knoll and walked among the graves, the light giving the stones a strange amber hue. She made her way to Margaret's grave and knelt beside it. She felt a closeness now, a kinship. Slowly, drawn to it, she moved over the grave and gently lay down on the sunken ground. She looked straight up through the trees at the red sky and ran her hands on the sloping sides, feeling cradled by the ground. The blanket of leaves beneath her comforted her, and she felt as if she were being rocked softly back and forth.

The girl came to her then and stood perfectly still with the child wrapped in the blanket. Lydia wanted to see the infant, to hold it even. She reached an arm out above her, opened her hand, and waited. The girl bent over the child, took it into herself, then turned slightly and faded. Lydia let her arm drop.

Is dead. She remembered the words. She said them to herself, then remembered other words. *Women have always lost children. It is a part of our heritage, our legacy. I am not the first.*

She took the words into herself, absorbed them the way the now yellowed pages had once absorbed the thick black ink, until they were no longer just words but something solid and whole that found its own place inside her.

She lay quietly for some time, listening to the sounds of the woods, then rose and pushed herself up out of the sunken ground and stood beside the grave. She read the stone a final time and turned and walked down from the graveyard toward home.